I0729651

Running for it

USA TODAY BESTSELLING AUTHOR

ALLYSON LINDT

To every geek girl,
everywhere,
be kind to yourself.

Chapter One

There's one thing the stories about Cinderella never mentioned—any prince who threw a ball and invited the entire city, just to find his bride, knew exactly how to appeal to the public.

The way Ramsey Miller worked the socialites in the Hotel America ballroom, with a warm smile here, a handshake there, and the occasional kiss on the cheek, was *Prince Charming*, brought to life.

He'd bleached the copper out of his hair—I assumed because blond polled better than auburn, or something ridiculous like that. He looked incredible anyway, wearing an easy smile and a suit made to accentuate his strong arms and torso.

I turned my attention back to my other guests, which was the reason I couldn't fault Ramsey too much for sweet-talking everyone tonight. This was *my* event, and even I intended to schmooze a little.

I'd rather have the check-equivalent of everything donated to the fundraiser, from the food to the hotel itself. But people had paid a good price for the meal, and would drop even more during the silent auction.

A trending hashtag always drew in more money than simply asking people to write a check. An event like this would ensure the kids who needed a place to stay, the residents of the LGBTQ+ shelter I ran, would have food and clothes, plus a little more, for the next several months. Nights like tonight produced ninety percent of the money that kept us afloat.

My sister never had this choice, which I still regretted years later. At least this way other kids like her would.

It wasn't my shelter—I hadn't founded it or anything—but over my years of volunteering, people had come and gone, until I was responsible for more and more. I wasn't technically even in charge, but we'd never been able to find a replacement after our last head left, so I did the job. Tonight, that included raising funds. Tomorrow, it might mean I was making lunch. Every day was a new experience.

"Violet." Lyn joined me near the wall, where I was recharging before my next pass through the room. "Amazing turnout."

"It really is. Better than I could have hoped for." When I wasn't working at the shelter, I managed Lyn's anime gaming café.

running for it

She was a great boss and good person, and these days, she practically glowed with happiness. At least a little bit of that had to do with her boyfriends—yes, plural. She had two, and I couldn't even imagine one making me that happy. I liked her guys, but they happened to be close friends with Ramsey, which was the only reason he was in my life again.

Lyn handed me a champagne glass with bubbly amber liquid in it. "Sparkling grape juice," she said. "How are you holding up?"

I loved *doing.* Working. Making a difference. Helping people. However, I preferred to do so behind the scenes or one-on-one. "Drained. But it's worth it."

"How appropriately direct." Lyn laughed lightly.

I smiled. "And true. The reminder keeps me going."

"I get that." Lyn nodded across the room, at Ramsey. "Do you need me to run interference?"

Even though he was around more often, Lyn did a good job of making sure I could be somewhere else when he came into the café. I think she misunderstood my reasons for wanting to stay away—not that I'd gone out of my way to set the record straight.

It wasn't that I didn't like Ramsey, though I tended to get defensive when he was around. It was that I remembered how good things were when I was with him. I adored the person he was behind closed doors. I even had fond—*scorching*—memories of those occasional nights we'd shared the bed with his best friend.

But he wasn't the same person in public. He was plastic. Fake. Working the world with a smile, a handshake, and the occasional kiss on the cheek.

"I'm good," I said to Lyn. "He's another guest tonight, and the last thing he wants is to draw attention to our past." It was the last thing I wanted too, but I wasn't going to wear a mask, in order to achieve it. I'd be polite, but I refused to be fake, even here.

Lyn gently squeezed my arm. "I'm going to find the guys. If you need anything, wave or holler or quack really loudly."

I chuckled. "I will." We both knew I wouldn't. I had this under control. My gaze drifted back to Ramsey, who gave me a tentative smile when he saw me. I turned away, not able to ignore the way my pulse kicked up.

Yup. Totally had this under control.

As Lyn melted back into the crowd, I swallowed the last of the sparkling juice, wheezing at the burn of bubbles down the back of my throat. Time to go thank more donors.

running for it

In my off-the-shoulder satin dress, and shoes and clutch dyed the exact same sapphire blue, I looked like I belonged with these people, in this world of crystal and sequins and diamonds.

But my dress was off the clearance rack, and my best friend, Luna, and I had turned our hands blue dying the accessories.

I was so out of place.

The politeness and platitudes flowed, as I said *hello* to one person after another.

"You've done a fantastic job with this event. You're so efficient."

"Those poor kids. Someone needs to show them love. They're lucky to have you."

"Did you put this entire thing together? I need to hire you to plan my next event."

I never quite knew what to say in return.

"Thanks. When our robot overlords take over, I plan to be their favorite human."

"They should thank the genie I told I wanted to spend my life helping people. I freed her after that."

"I run on caffeine and fresh day-planner pages. Are you sure you can afford my rates?"

All of it said in jest, though from the expressions I got in return, most of the people here didn't do *jesting*. The best responses I got were giggles and *you're silly*.

When I was dating Ramsey, I jokingly referred to myself once as Laffy Taffy. Frequently stale, just a little off flavor, and always ready with a horrible pun.

He'd corrected me. Told me I was more like saltwater taffy. I was sweet, fun to unwrap, came in the best flavors, and was his favorite.

"You're a hard woman to track down. Most popular person here."

Hunter's voice behind me promised real conversation and summoned memories I liked to ignore. The kind that sent delicious shivers running down my spine, along with the ghost of his fingertips over my skin. Because those times when he'd joined Ramsey and me...

"Everybody wants a piece of me. What can I say?" I winced as the words passed my lips. He was totally going to take that wrong. I spun to find him standing there with Ramsey, and a tribe of butterflies leapt to life in my stomach.

"Can't say I blame them." Laughter danced in Ramsey's green eyes. His presence made my heart whimper.

Hunter was just as breathtaking. Dark hair. Strong jaw. Long, skilled fingers.

I swallowed the lust surging through me. "Thank you for coming this evening, gentlemen. Your support means a lot to the kids."

running for it

Hunter snorted in disbelief. "Did you just feed us a prepared line? Who are you, and what have you done with Violet?"

"I learned it from watching you." I smiled sweetly. "Thought I'd communicate in your language." Which was what I needed to remember. I'd pushed them out of my life because after a while, the stark difference between their public and private personas became too stressful to be around.

"Don't we feel special?" Ramsey's tone was playful. "I won't hold you up. We just wanted to say *hi* and congratulate you on a fabulous event."

I turned up my smile. "Thank you. I'm going to pretend you mean that."

"I do, Ta—" Ramsey shook his head.

Taffy. The pet name tugged at my heart. I didn't do *phony* with anyone, and I'd just about reached my limit here. "Enjoy your evening." I walked away before I could say something I'd regret in the morning. Like, *Maybe we could try again.*

I tried to get back into the mingling, but every time I turned, I either saw Ramsey or Hunter, or was disappointed that I didn't.

This wasn't great.

As the event wound down, Hunter joined me again. "Fair warning. Don't jump to conclusions; Ramsey promised to behave."

My stomach lurched. "What does that mean?"

"Can I have everyone's attention?" Ramsey's voice carried from the center of the ballroom. He stepped onto a chair.

What was this? Morbid curiosity kept my feet frozen to the ground.

"Violet has been thanking each of you individually, but I want everyone to know how grateful I am—*she is*—that you're all here tonight. This is such an important cause, and your support means the world to these kids." Ramsey commanded attention without even trying, and looked and sounded good doing so.

But— "This isn't so bad."

"Excuse me. Hi." A woman stepped up next to him. "Hello." She waved at the crowd.

Hunter sighed, and when I looked at him, his jaw was clenched.

It wasn't over.

"Ramsey's too humble to say, but I'm hoping I see even half of this generosity when I call each of you for campaign donations." She laughed lightly. *Tittered*—I finally understood what that word meant.

Did she just— Who the hell was this woman, hijacking my event? Was she really begging for funds for Ramsey's State Senate campaign, now?

"Thank you, Debbie." Ramsey's voice was tight. "But Violet doesn't need us hijacking her event. That's the peak of tacky." Though he sounded

running for it

cool. I saw the anger flashing in his eyes. But if she were a member of his staff, saying more would make him look bad.

"Violet…" Hunter was apologetic.

I yanked away from his hand on my arm. "Nope. Don't bother. In fact, tell Ramsey it's lovely to see nothing has changed." I let disappointment spill into my retort. I needed this kind of visceral reminder of why I kept him at arm's length.

Chapter Two

If there was a mood for so-completely-unsurprised-I-couldn't-be-angry, that was me. At least, that was what I tried to convince myself of, as I sat at a table in the back of the ballroom, working through numbers and paperwork for the night. My shoes sat next to me on the table, taunting me with their cruel heels and the torture they'd done to my feet tonight.

The hotel staff had cleanup under control, and technically this could wait until morning. But it was going to take me a little while to shut off my brain, to keep it from focusing on the moment I was pretending I didn't care about, so I might as well get something done while I was here.

The chair next to me slid out, and the familiar scent of ice and musk greeted me. I wouldn't give Ramsey the satisfaction of looking up.

"How's my favorite workaholic?" His voice was warm.

I grabbed my handbag and opened the side pocket.

running for it

"What are you doing?" Ramsey asked.

I handed him a small make-up mirror. "Letting you talk to your favorite workaholic."

"She's got a point." Hunter dropped into a seat across the table.

Nope. I wasn't getting sucked into banter with them, especially not after what happened earlier. "Have a good evening." I closed my tablet and stood to leave.

"Wait."

Ramsey's hand on my arm stalled me as much as his request.

He rose as well. "Let me apologize." The playfulness was gone.

I shook my head. "Please don't. Not if it's going to happen again." And it would. "I'm not mad. I should have expected it."

Ramsey tightened his grip. "It won't. I was furious Debbie did this. She's fantastic at her job, but she's also new and doesn't know all our rhythms yet. I've talked to her. It wasn't right of her to hijack your event, and I'm sincerely sorry."

"Okay." I tugged out of his grasp and crossed my arms. This was where I should leave, so why was I still here? Because all night, my defenses had been slipping. He'd taken steps to fix things, and this wasn't specifically his fault. "So… how have you been?" I hid my wince at my weak question.

Hunter smiled. "Small talk. I think you broke her."

I stuck my tongue out at him.

"Don't offer unless you mean it." Hunter winked.

I rolled my eyes but couldn't hide my amusement. Sticking around put me in a tough situation, though. Hunter was right that I hated small talk, but I didn't want to get sucked into a real conversation with them either. *Just leave.* "I caught Ravyn's latest comic. I love where she's taking the series." Ravyn was Ramsey's twin sister.

"She got the imagination in the family," Hunter teased.

"I don't need talent when I'm this good looking." Ramsey gestured at himself. "Besides, you weren't complaining about my imagination the other night." His gaze was on Hunter. Were they flirting with each other?

I'd seen them together in the bedroom—the whole friends-with-benefits thing Ramsey and I had with Hunter—but not *together,* as in a couple. "Any secrets about where the story's going?" I asked. "Insider information?"

Hunter covered his ears. "No spoilers."

Damn them, I was enjoying this.

"You'd rather talk about my sister than about me?" Ramsey's hurt was exaggerated.

running for it

"I figure that'll get me more answers than asking about you." Catty? A little.

"I'll tell you anything you want to know," he said.

I couldn't ignore his sincerity. Then again, that had never quite been the problem. He had always been genuine with me, but the mask he put on for public consumption was a different person, and I didn't like watching him flip that switch.

"Do you still play?" I asked. It wasn't a secret that he could play guitar, but he didn't tell anyone that when he was younger, he wanted to be in a metal band. He composed music, and Hunter wrote the lyrics.

"I do. In fact, we've been working on something for a couple of weeks. Stress relief."

"Can I hear?" The question was out before I could consider that I was falling into this conversation and enjoying it. I wouldn't take the request back, though. I always enjoyed their collaborations.

Ramsey leaned in, mouth near enough my ear I felt his breath on my skin, and sang. The lyrics were angsty, and his voice had that rough edge so many metal singers wished for. When Hunter sang as he stood, picking up the harmony, chills raced down my spine.

"I love it. It's heartbreaking and beautiful."

Hunter worked his jaw, then shook his head. "What?"

"I was going to say, *Your face is heartbreaking and beautiful,* but I wasn't sure how you'd take it."

I ducked my head. *Your-face* exchanges were typical for us back in the day, but the comment flustered me.

"Not used to seeing you at a loss for words," Hunter said.

"I hope you're pleased with yourself." Great. Now *I* was starting to get flirty.

"Whoa. My best friend and my ex? Not. Cool." Ramsey's tone was light and playful, with zero trace of offense.

Any time I'd seen Ramsey in the past few months, Lyn or someone else was around. Having witnesses made it easier to stick to my resolve to keep my distance. But now, no one else was here.

This was half-fun, half-awkward, and all-enticing. Did I want to fall into it, or walk away? "You know you'd watch." Fall into it, apparently, because now those tantalizing memories were back, refusing to be ignored while they sent desire spilling through me.

"He absolutely would," Hunter agreed.

Ramsey hadn't moved away from me since he finished singing. "I don't know. It's *so hard* to picture myself in that situation." He pressed into my

running for it

back. "A person never really knows what they're going to do, until the situation actually presents itself."

Hunter made a lassoing gesture—Jr. Rodeo Champion three years in a row—and mimed pulling himself closer to us. He wrapped an arm around my waist and dipped me. My squeal of surprise vanished when he paused with his lips a breath from mine.

My pulse hammered in my veins and roared in my ears.

Ramsey cleared his throat. "I don't think I could watch." His tone was impossible to decipher.

"Never bothered you before." Hunter righted me, taking his time before pulling away.

Ramsey grasped my fingers and tugged, to spin me into his arms. He gripped the back of my neck and held my gaze. "Watching definitely wouldn't work for me. I'd have to participate."

I was one hundred percent heat and desire. "If you're not careful, I might think the two of you are serious." My voice came out thicker and huskier than I intended.

"What do I have to do to convince you we are?" Ramsey asked.

My breath caught. Goddess, I could drown in that gaze.

"I've got a room here for the night." His voice was low. "Bed big enough for three."

"We're not getting back together." I had to put that out there now, before I lost all grip on my senses.

Ramsey hovered his mouth near enough mine I felt his breath on my skin. "Tell me you don't still feel that spark."

"Just one night." I was reminding myself as much as them.

"Not *just*." Hunter was at my back. "It'll be so incredible you won't forget."

I never had. I rose on my toes, to press my lips to Ramsey's.

He gripped my neck harder, and crushed his mouth to mine. I gasped in disappointment when Ramsey broke away too quickly for my liking, but he didn't let me go.

He pressed his forehead to mine. "We should continue this conversation upstairs," he said in that same growly voice he sang in.

The sound and sentiment were a skilled touch, sliding over me. "If you insist."

The three of us left the ballroom, walking side by side but not touching. I'd be wounded by that, but there was no reason to announce a casual hookup to the world. Besides, the anticipation that roared through me was wonderful at helping me ignore most everything except what came next.

The elevator ride up was quiet. Cool. From the outside, three friends sharing a car up to their

running for it

respective rooms. The stroll down the hallway was the same.

Ramsey opened the door with a sleight of hand so smooth he would have made most magicians jealous, and let us in the room. I caught a glimpse of sprawling luxury, before his hands were on my cheeks and my back was against the wall. He kissed me hard, devouring my moans and clinging to me like I was his oxygen. Or that was me, arms around his neck and nails digging into his shoulders, clinging for all I had.

Chapter Three

I lost track of one kiss flowing into the next and then another. At any other time, I could deny how much I missed this—how much I missed Ramsey—but not now. This was familiar. Delicious. Everything.

When Ramsey let me go, I didn't have time to flounder, before Hunter was tilting my head in his direction. Claiming my lips. Knotting his fingers in my hair. I swore sparks danced everywhere he touched. He and I had always connected—that whole friends-with-benefits thing—but tonight, it felt more intense.

Maybe I was making more of this than I should be. On the other hand, my memory had understated the feeling of Ramsey's fingers gliding up my arms. His breath on my skin. Hunter's teasing growl, as he licked a line up my neck.

Ramsey slid my zipper down my back one agonizing tooth at a time. "I missed unwrapping my favorite candy." He drew his mouth up my shoulder

running for it

to my neck, and then to nibble on my ear. "You taste even sweeter than I remember."

"My second wish from the genie. *Make me candy flavored.*" It didn't matter that I hadn't had that conversation with them earlier; they ran with the reference.

"Your face is candy flavored." Hunter caught my bottom lip between his teeth.

I laughed. I'd missed both of them, not just Ramsey. "One of the things I like about you. You're not going to follow that with, *So's my cock. Want a taste?*"

Hunter rolled his eyes. "Tacky. Besides, you already know it's more of a cherry flavor."

"It's true." My teasing faded into a surprised gasp when something fitted over my eyes.

Ramsey pressed his lips into the hollow behind my ear. "Since you're only here for the night, let's make the most of it." He pushed my dress to the ground, leaving me blind and exposed, in nothing but a strapless bra and panties.

My anticipation was back, spiking my pulse and making my head fuzzier than any champagne could. Fingers grasped mine and tugged, all other contact falling away. I didn't hesitate to follow. I trusted whoever led me to do so safely.

Another pair of hands rested on my hips and pulled me to a stop. My bra fell away, and my panties were pushed to the ground. Cool air kissed my dampness, and my heart hammered against my ribs.

"On the bed. On your back." Ramsey set my hand on the edge of the mattress, so I'd know where it was.

I didn't make any excuses or apologies for loving the way he took charge in the bedroom. The last few years apart, the arguments since—they all fell away as I did as commanded.

Silence settled into the room, blanketing me in desire and raising goosebumps everywhere. With no sight, I strained my ears for any indication of where they were. Of what came next.

Hands grabbed my wrists and pinned them above my head.

Ramsey's lips on mine drew a light moan. I didn't need to see, to know who was kissing me; he was more demanding, serious, and eternally clean shaven. He followed a lazy path down my chest. He paused to flick his tongue over my nipples until I squirmed against Hunter's grip, then continued his journey downward.

Ramsey kissed over my stomach. Lower. Dropped to kiss my leg near my knee.

It didn't matter how much I struggled or groaned; I wasn't getting free. The anticipation was delicious.

running for it

His journey back up was more excruciating. He bit the inside of my thigh, and I groaned at the spike of pleasure mingled with the sting of pain. When he finally reached the focus of my need and dragged his tongue up my pussy, my hips rose off the bed, wanting to be closer.

Hunter cupped my breast and kneaded it, rolling a nipple between his fingers.

Ramsey licked feverishly, gliding up to my clit but not making contact, before driving his tongue deep inside me. He tasted and teased, until I was whimpering, before he finally wrapped a finger on either side of my clit, and sucked the swollen bud.

I came hard, pressing into his mouth. He didn't let up, even after I slumped back against the mattress. He dove two fingers inside me, still tracing the alphabet over my clit, pushing me past discomfort and into another orgasm.

Hunter's grip fell away, and he pressed his lips to my shoulder. "You good?"

I nodded. "So good." My throat was raw. Had I been screaming?

Ramsey slid between my legs, the friction of flesh on flesh dancing through every hyper-aware nerve ending. He nudged my opening, then thrust inside me, stretching me out as he buried himself to the hilt.

My breath came in shallow gasps, as he glided out to the tip before thrusting back in and working to a steady rhythm.

Hunter pressed his cock to my lips, and I parted to let him in.

Ramsey picked up the pace, until he slammed against me hard and frantic. Hunter didn't stay in my mouth much. Their groans and touches were a new layer of eroticism, pushing me toward another climax but not over the edge.

Hunter's grunts shifted, and I knew he was coming. My body remembered all these sounds. Scents. Sensations. Tastes as that first salty spurt hit the back of my throat, and he emptied himself in my mouth.

Goddess, I'd missed this.

The mattress near my head shifted, and then by my shoulders and side, as Hunter moved next to me.

Lips wrapped around one of my nipples, and Hunter flicked with his tongue. He sought out my clit, teasing and coaxing while Ramsey fucked me.

I lost track of where one feeling ended and the next one started, as I tumbled into another orgasm. Ramsey's grip on my legs, his punctuated groans, told me he was there too.

My world spun in the best way possible, though the ride had stopped. I was lost in a cloud of post-coital amazingness.

running for it

Ramsey loosened the blindfold and tugged me onto my side, as he lay facing me. He kissed the tip of my nose. "Missed you, Taffy."

"I missed you too." It didn't change anything, but there was no reason to get into reality right now. We'd established rules before we started, and the world would still be waiting in the morning.

I was vaguely aware of the mattress shifting. This wasn't my pillow or my sheets, but I knew that scent…

"I'll talk to you in a few hours." That was Ramsey's whisper.

I reluctantly pried one eye open, to find a fully dressed Ramsey pulling away from Hunter and standing.

"What's wrong? What time is it?" Sleep slurred my words and my brain.

Ramsey moved to my side of the bed. "It's barely four. Go back to sleep." His tone was soft and kind.

"But—"

He brushed his lips over mine. "I have an early meeting, but there's no reason you have to be up yet. Sleep. Enjoy the room." He kissed me lightly again. "Last night was amazing."

Warm fuzzies flitted in my chest and wrapped me in warmth. I wouldn't ask if we could do it again, but the words were right there.

"See you both later." And Ramsey was gone.

What wasn't he saying? The desire to sleep, plus the lingering feeling of security, wouldn't let me focus on the question.

"Come on. I'm tired. You're comfortable." Hunter wrapped an arm around my waist and pulled me back into him.

The touch was familiar. Safe. Hunter had been a good friend and was a brilliant cuddler. It wasn't like I was going to make a habit of this, so it wouldn't hurt to finish out the night here.

"You're ringing." Hunter's sleepy voice dragged me awake again.

The numbers on the clock taunted my blurry gaze. "Your face is ringing." Not my best comeback, but it was five in the morning.

"That doesn't even make sense." Hunter extracted himself from the bed.

Your face doesn't make sense. Nope. I was awake enough now that no longer sounded clever. I sat up, took my purse from him when he handed it over, and extracted my phone.

Luna. If she were calling instead of texting, it couldn't be good. "Hello?"

running for it

"Violet? You need to get here now. There's water everywhere, and it's so hot, and—oh God—I don't know what to do." Panic rang heavy in her voice.

Chapter Four

I adored Luna. She was my best friend and frequently my link to sanity. She wasn't always great under pressure, though.

One of last night's shelter volunteers called in, and as she frequently did, Luna offered to step in. She was more of a night owl, especially since she was having trouble finding a steady job in her field, so she promised it was no problem.

"Luna"—I kept my tone kind but firm—"take a deep breath. What's going on?" *There's water everywhere*, sounded far less serious than, *There's blood everywhere,* so I wasn't ready to panic.

Luna sighed. "The boiler broke. Or exploded. Or something. What do boilers do? It's leaking. The basement is flooding. Why is the water a nasty color? That's not normal. The kids are freaking ou—"

"*Luna.*" This was so not what I needed this morning. Not that it was her fault, or that I wanted something like this on any morning, but today I'd hoped to spend a couple more hours wrapped in warm fuzzy memories before I had to face reality.

running for it

"The water shut-off valve is under the stairs, in the wall. Turn it off. Have Oliver help you if it's stuck. I'll be there in twenty minutes."

"Okay. And Violet? Thank you." She already sounded less panicked.

I smiled at the genuine gratitude. When I disconnected, I found Hunter watching me with a mix of amusement and concern.

"I'm guessing whatever that was, it means you don't have time for breakfast," he said.

An ache of regret pinged in my chest. "No. Crisis at the shelter." I climbed out of bed and paused, suddenly hyper aware of my lack of clothes. What was I doing? He'd held me down and fucked my face last night, and I cared if he saw me naked this morning?

Apparently so.

He didn't seem to have the same hang-up, as he stood at the foot of the bed gloriously naked.

Goddess, he was handsome.

I forced aside the sudden burst of modesty, and gathered my clothes. My panties were a wreck, but I could go without. The strapless bra would be less than comfortable, but it would do for now. "*Fuck*," I muttered when I grabbed the dress.

"What's wrong?" Hunter had pulled on a pair of boxers. That was moderately better, but no less distracting.

I held up the dress. "Not exactly made for flood clean-up, and I don't have time to go home." I didn't care if anyone saw me in last night's clothes, but wet, skin-tight satin would be impossible to work in. Worse, if it ripped, I'd expose my panty-less ass to a house full of teenagers.

"I got you." Hunter rummaged through a suitcase near the bed.

The last thing I wanted was to be in something of Ramsey's. "I'll be—" I stopped when Hunter straightened and handed me a Westminster College T-shirt and a pair of jogging shorts.

Ramsey went to the U, like any proud local boy whose family's name was on at least one of the school's buildings. I know—I met him in college. I was there on an academic scholarship. He wasn't.

These were Hunter's clothes.

Only slightly less awkward, and far more curious, but I needed something. "Thank you." I took the clothes from him and tugged them on. They were a few sizes too big, but drawstrings on the shorts kept them up, and a knot at the waist of the shirt prevented it from turning me into a human sail.

"I thought this was Ramsey's room." That he was only in for one night.

Was that hesitation? "It is," Hunter said. "But we've been doing a lot of strategy planning for the primaries, so I made myself at home."

running for it

Sounded reasonable, but I felt like there was more to the story. An unformed question tickled my tongue.

My phone chimed. The text from Luna just read, *SOS. It's getting worse.*

"I need to go." I grabbed my purse. "Where are my shoes?"

We spent a moment searching for them, but they were nowhere to be found.

How did I lose my shoes? It didn't matter, since I couldn't work in the heels anyway. I'd buy a pair of slippers in the hotel gift shop and borrow someone's shoes when I got to the shelter. I was out of time. "Thank you. For *everything*."

Hunter squeezed my fingers. "Any time. Good luck. Call me if you need anything."

"I will." I wouldn't.

On the elevator ride down, I raked my fingers through my hair and pulled it back into a ponytail. It was early enough the lobby was nearly empty. Fortunately, I had the day off from Loading Java because of last night's event, so I didn't have to let Lyn down by calling in.

I dialed the emergency plumber as I drove, and made arrangements to get someone out to the shelter in the next couple of hours.

Any other calls would have to wait until I saw the actual damage.

I pulled into the small strip of asphalt on the side of the building—aka the *parking lot*. Luna's car was here, along with a few belonging to the residents. There wasn't room for more.

The shelter was actually a converted pair of houses, some of the oldest in the city. A polygamist had built on the adjoining properties for his two wives, with a corridor connecting the homes, so he could more easily split his time between his families.

The main house was on the corner of the block, and that was where the entrance was, as well. I walked in, to find the main common area strewn with mattresses, water pooling around each, creating a series of mini lakes on the hardwood.

"The basement is flooded," Luna explained. "So I had the mattresses brought up here."

We were more crowded than normal due to the cold weather, so there were temporary rooms downstairs.

I couldn't complain that she'd started on cleanup, even if the results weren't quite ideal. The situation was shitty, regardless. I pointed at a couple of older teenagers. "You, haul these outside and stack them near the dumpster." I singled out another lurker. "Grab the mop, ring it out in the bucket, and get as much water as you can."

The bulk of the damage would be in the basement, but I needed to do a quick tour of the rest

running for it

of the house, to make sure every room that needed attention got it.

The main floor was common area, with several tables, chairs, and sofas, for people to gather and be social. The other house held the kitchen and dining room.

It was the top two floors that made this shelter different from the larger, state-funded ones. The smaller, original bedrooms were still intact and slept two people each. I did a quick survey of the individual rooms, careful not to invade any more of the residents' privacy than I needed to.

Since we only allowed minors here who had left home or had been kicked out due to their sexual orientation or identity, we wanted to give them a new home. A place where they could go without worrying for their safety, so they could get back to life and growing up.

That also meant everyone helped out, because this was their home.

My sister, Eva had been ten years younger than me, so I was gone and out on my own before she hit her teens. She and I hadn't been close enough for her to come to me when she started struggling with her sexuality.

Instead, she'd gone to our parents. The people who should have protected and loved us. They sent her to conversion therapy, and less than two weeks in, she'd taken her life.

I never forgave them or myself. But at least here, these kids would have the kind of acceptance she hadn't.

The upstairs was undamaged by today's event. A few of the rooms looked like hurricanes had blown through, but that was status quo. A chill was setting in, though, and an overall musty smell permeated the building.

I told everyone to bundle up, to grab clothes from next door if they needed layers, and promised the heat would be back soon.

"How can I help?" Jesse—one of our older guys—leaned against his doorframe. Dark circles were under eyes that bugged out when he tried to hide his cough. He'd been sick for a couple days but refused to rest. There was always something more he felt he *had* to do.

I pointed him back into the room. "You can get some sleep. I'm ordering you."

His chuckle faded in a cough. "You ever take your own advice to slow down and let others help?"

"Nope. And when you're in charge, you can exempt yourself from the rules."

"If growing up means working myself to the bone, no thanks," someone behind me said.

running for it

I turned to kindly shoo them away, but they'd already run off.

Basement next. I took a few deep breaths, to steel myself for what I'd find, and headed in.

The water was almost up to the bottom step.

I hollered four names and handed out more tasks. "Grab some tarps from the toolshed. One goes at the top of the stairs, one out under the pavilion. Two of you haul boxes up the stairs and set them on the first tarp, the other two finish taking the boxes outside. The moment you're done, out of the wet clothes and into extra layers, to warm up."

I hated asking them. If any of them got sick because of this, I'd feel so bad. But the work needed to be done quickly.

While I picked my way through the basement to make sure I hadn't missed anything, cold biting into my ankles, I called the place we got our beds from. They'd have replacement mattresses for me in a couple of days.

It was too long—we were already past capacity—but yelling wasn't going to magically increase the available supply.

My phone rang, and I answered. The plumber was running behind. Go figure. I had a basement full of water, and he had more important things to deal with.

I could call other places, but I'd worked with this one enough that I trusted them and they gave us a good rate.

"If you have a sump pump, you can start getting the water out before I get there," he said. "I'll do it once I arrive, if you haven't, but this will make things go faster."

"Where am I supposed to get a sump pump?" I was asking myself as much as him.

"I-bet-Oz-has-one." Luna's rush of words startled me, and I spun to find her standing at the bottom of the stairs. Pink dotted her cheeks, probably not all from the cold.

Cole—he only let Luna call him Oz—had a hard exterior and a soft heart. He'd been a huge name in tech more than a decade ago, but decided he was tired of the grind. One of his rentals had a lot of basement-flooding problems because the property sat on a water table.

He was also a beast of a grump with almost everyone but Luna. Who would be happy to call him, based on the way she was biting her bottom lip.

"I'll get started on water removal," I told the plumber. "Get here as soon as you can."

The plumber sighed. "You should know, if anything big is broken, I can't start work today anyway. Your boiler is so old, there's a good chance

running for it

I'll need to order parts. It's going to be a couple of days."

So I had a house over full of people, without enough beds and with no heat.

Wonderful.

Chapter Five

I made some calls, to get space heaters. It took calls to five different places to find enough heaters, but I secured them all.

"Cole's here." Luna practically lit up at the sound of an old truck parking on the street.

I followed her around front. Cole's pickup was an ancient Chevy with a hardtop, with as many parts replaced as were original. I waved at Cole, and he gave me a terse nod. His gaze flitted past me quickly, to land on Luna. As he turned back to his pickup, I swore I saw the corner of his mouth twitch.

"Brought some stuff." He opened the camper shell and tailgate.

He pulled out a couple of giant fans.

"Eep." Luna squealed. "You're amazing. Basement is soaked. Wet carpet everywhere. Does that sound dirty? Didn't mean it that way. Promise."

Cole glanced at her with a raised eyebrow, then grabbed more things from his truck. A bucket, some PVC pipe, and what I assumed was the pump. "This

running for it

is temporary. It'll get you cleaned out. Let you know when I'm done," he said.

"Do you need help? That's a lot of stuff." Luna was already reaching for the bucket.

Cole moved it out of her range. "I got it."

Luna didn't look wounded by his gruffness. "Okay."

"I could use some help." I felt bad pulling her away from Cole, with as excited as she looked, but this was best for all of us. "I need to sift through the stuff that's under the pavilion."

"Of course." Luna had recovered from her earlier stress, and I assumed it had something to do with the well-muscled, grumbly man standing a few feet away.

"Find me when you're done," I said to Cole.

He nodded.

Luna waved at his back, as I gently tugged her toward the yard. When we got there, she nodded at my T-shirt. "Westminster?"

Last night rushed back to me in a poofy cloud of pleasant memories. It tugged along a reminder that my past with Ramsey and Luna was messy. I was torn between giving her all the naughty details, the way I normally would, or keeping them to myself because of *who* they involved. "I didn't make it home last night," I confessed.

Luna let out an exaggerated gasp. "Was he cute? Well hung? All of the above, I'm sure. Probably smart."

"All of the above." I pointed her toward a box. "If it's salvageable, set it on a table. If it's unrecognizable, throw it out. If you're not sure, ask me. We'll decide. How'd your interview go yesterday afternoon?" Probably didn't end in a job, since Luna hadn't called me, but that didn't mean it went badly. Few interviews resulted in on-the-spot offers.

Shit. I shouldn't have mentioned her search for jobs. That would tie back to Ramsey, as well. But I did want to know, and between yesterday's event and this morning's crisis…

"It was all right." Luna's tone implied it wasn't great. "I got through all the questions. They seemed really impressed with my credentials and my test results."

"But…?"

"But then one of the interviewers asked me if I was *that* Luna. It's not a common name or anything…" Her shoulders slumped, and she dove back into her work.

Luna was a brilliant programmer. Yeah, I was biased, but it went beyond that. When we were in college, Luna had worked with a professor to build a *cure* for one of the most malicious pieces of malware

running for it

the internet had seen in about five years. Her code had saved hundreds of schools that had been held hostage billions of dollars.

The problem was, the last virus that was as bad, a few years earlier, was hers. She hadn't done it maliciously. A lot of people might not believe that, but I knew Luna. She'd done it because someone said, *Hey, I bet you can't do this*, and she said, *That sounds like fun. I bet I can.* She'd done it for the challenge, never stopping to think someone would do evil things with it.

When various international law enforcement agencies caught up with her for the earlier code, that was what she became known for. No one cared about the good she'd done since.

"I'm sorry, L." I wished I could do something for her.

"I expect it. When it goes better, it'll taste so much sweeter. And it will go better." She shrugged again. "Don't think you can dodge the question. Does your Westminster boy know you're a U girl?"

"Lots of people wear Westminster shirts, not just alumni. And none of them care where I went to school." The entire box I was looking through was clothing, caked in mud. Cheaper to replace through donations, than to get these back to wearable again. I carried it to the *toss* pile.

When I turned back to Luna, she was watching me with wide eyes, her mouth in an *O* shape. "You hooked up with Hunter." Her voice echoed off concrete and aluminum.

"I di— What? Why would you say that?"

"Because you're making a big deal out of a T-shirt, and he's the only reason you would."

"I'm not making a big deal out of anything. I didn't even mention it." I couldn't deny her guess though. I couldn't lie to Luna.

"Mhm." Her serious expression melted to a grin when she opened a box of books and flipped through a few without any pages sticking together from water damage. She moved each clean book with reverence, giving the pile an isolated spot on the table. "Does Ramsey know?"

I sucked on my teeth, searching for the right way to say *definitely yes*. She knew I'd been with both of them before. My breakup with Ramsey had directly and specifically coincided with Luna's legal issues.

"I see. That sounds fun. Was it fun?" Luna's question was strained.

My heart sank. "I'm sorry. It wasn't— I shouldn't have— It's not like it's going to happen again." I'd discovered early on in dating Ramsey that I struggled with his two halves—public and private. I was willing to overlook it most of the time,

running for it

especially when we first hooked up. The sex was amazing, the conversation was amazing, *Ramsey* was amazing. So what if he'd been raised to be polite in mixed company?

"Why not?"

The question caught me off guard, and I struggled to wrap my brain around it. "We broke up." It was the not-so-polite, upper-class company Ramsey kept that I started to have an issue with. The off-color jokes were nothing new. When we were in college, Luna and I spent a lot of time at parties, and I'd heard plenty of crude jokes and comments about my various body parts.

The more time I spent around friends of Ramsey's family, the less tolerable they got. The worst part was Ramsey would laugh along with them.

"Because of me." Luna stopped sorting. She was frowning now. "You still care about him. You miss him. You go out of your way to prove to yourself that you don't, but you do. And it's because of me."

"No. What happened with you was a catalyst, but it wasn't the cause. I should have left him long before that." Things started to deteriorate when the jokes turned toward me. My decisions.

"That's a sexy piece of ass. You plan on sharing her before you make her yours forever?"

"You ever worry she spends so much time with those kids?"

"You oughta lock her away before she starts thinking she can change the world."

Those were the nice things. What hurt the most was that Ramsey never shut them down, and he actively worked to keep me from doing so. He'd apologize at home. *They don't know any better.* He never wanted to hear that they might if he told them or let me tell them.

And then Luna was arrested. The people around Ramsey never said her name, they didn't even know her, but her case was high profile in the business world.

"This is why you get them pregnant early. So they don't get all uppity."

"No way a pretty little thing like her was smart enough to do this."

"Face like that looks better with something in her mouth."

"Too bad she'll turn in prison. A woman like that needs a good man to straighten her out."

When I went off on them, Ramsey had to physically drag me from the room, apologizing for *my* behavior. After we left, he was sorry. It wasn't enough. I told him I couldn't do that anymore. He said I couldn't ask him to pick between me and the people who could make or break his career.

running for it

"It definitely wasn't your fault," I repeated to Luna.

She fiddled with a damp fringe on a pillow. "He's gotten better. Making a stand. Building his campaign on fixing some of these things. He was at the fundraiser."

"It's too late." My reply came out with less force than I intended.

We were finishing up the box sorting, when Cole came out and said he was ready to set up fans. Luna jumped to her feet to help him, and I let her.

I tried to ignore my inner war over Ramsey, as I found places for the new mattresses and set up the space heaters that were delivered. We were past capacity. I hated turning people away, but we couldn't take anyone else in.

When the plumber finally showed up, I breathed a sigh of relief. He spent about half an hour in the basement, before telling me he had to call someone else in.

That couldn't be good.

I stuck close, as he took his associate first through the basement and then through the rest of the house. It was hard to hear them, with their heads bent together and the whispered words, but they made a lot of notes.

When they turned back to me, they wore matching grim expressions.

"The boiler can't be fixed," the plumber said. "The best way to heat the place is going to be installing central air, especially in this climate, with this setup. The problem is, the house isn't built to support the ductwork."

"So… what do I need to do?" A nagging thought in the back of my mind was starting to panic, but I couldn't give it my attention.

They exchanged looks again, and the plumber handed me a tablet. "This is a breakdown of what we recommend. You're welcome to call around for other estimates. I understand. The thing is, the house isn't livable as a shelter as it is. If you can't bring it up to code in a week, we'll have to file to have the building condemned. And while the work is being done, we can't have anyone living here."

This couldn't be happening. What was I going to do? Fundraisers like the one last night brought in operating capital, not the kind of money it would take to renovate or get a whole new building. And even if we could raise the money, we had to deal with where the kids would stay until this place was overhauled or a new place was ready.

I needed time. Ideas. Money.

Connections.

Damn it. I needed Ramsey.

running for it

You're doing this for the kids, repeated in my head as I pulled up his personal number. The one no one had, except his closest friends and family.

"Hey, Taffy." The smile in his voice sent pleasant shivers racing down my spine whether or not I wanted it to. "Long time no talk."

The hint of playfulness should make this easier. It didn't.

"Hey." I dragged in a deep, silent breath. *This is for the kids*. "I… um… I-need-a-favor."

Silence.

Was this where he'd tease me? Give me grief about coming groveling, when I swore I'd never be one of those people who used their connections?

"Anything. What's wrong?" Damn him, for sounding concerned.

"I'm at the shelter. A city inspector just left." I'd keep this clinical and factual. More for my sake than his, since I was the one dreading this conversation. "He's condemning the building. I know you can't fix unsafe construction, but… I don't know what to do." It hurt to admit that. This call *was* my plan, and it was the best I had.

"I've got you covered. Give me the night, and I'll call you back tomorrow morning."

This would be okay. He'd help me figure things out. "Thank you."

Chapter Six

I woke up to a string of alerts on my phone, all with the shelter's name, as well as messages from another of the shelter volunteers. *There are cameras outside. A news van. What do I do?*

What?

I clicked through to the first alert. Local news, running a story about the shelter. About it shutting down. About all of these kids becoming homeless for a second time.

Every story was a flavor of the same.

This wasn't what I had in mind when I asked Ramsey for help.

I replied to the text. *Remind them the kids can't be on camera.* The last thing we needed was to get in trouble for exploiting minors. *Otherwise be polite. I'll let you know as soon as I have answers.*

I dialed Ramsey next. I was going to be cool, icy even, while I got to the bottom of why he thought this was the way to go.

"Taffy." He was chipper when he answered.

"What the fuck did you do?"

running for it

"Good morning, Ramsey," he said in a falsetto supposed to be me. "How did you sleep? *Goddess*, that one night we had together reminded me how much I love your cock."

I growled. The teasing used to be fun, but not now. "I have you on speaker. The cameraman wants to know if you're really that well hung." My words came out with more of an edge than Ramsey's had.

"Hmm. Be honest with him."

Fucker wasn't supposed to call my bluff. "You don't want that," I said.

"I'm not any more insecure about my dick size than you are likely to be talking to the press while you bitch me out."

I clenched my teeth. "You knew it would piss me off, and yet you called them anyway. What happened to talking in the morning? Making a plan together?" I pulled on clothes. Thankfully, I'd showered last night, to get rid of the swamp-water smell that permeated me.

"We're talking. I assume we'll be planning soon. I didn't ask you, because you would have said *no*."

I put him on speaker and set the phone on my bathroom counter, so I could yank a brush through my hair. "If you knew I wasn't going to like it, you shouldn't have done it."

He *tsk*ed. "You and I both know putting something in the public eye, exposing it, is what gets it attention. If you didn't think that, you wouldn't hold the fundraisers."

"So you couldn't have said this to me when we spoke last night, *before* you arranged it? I'm not unreasonable." I didn't have time for much makeup. A touch of lip gloss, a feather of mascara, and I was good.

"Time was critical, and I had to make a decision or miss the opportunity."

"Which was it, Ramsey?" I made my way to the kitchen. We had coffee at Lyn's place, and it was free, but I needed a kick to get me there. "You didn't have time to ask me, or you figured it easier to ask forgiveness than permission?"

"A little of both. Hang on. Tell them I'll be there in fifteen. Yeah, it's her." His last two statements were distant, as if he'd pulled the phone from his ear. "Sorry about that. Hunter says *hi*."

Suspicion snaked through me, and I set the empty coffee pot on the counter. "Fifteen minutes to what? Where are you?"

"The shelter. Someone needs to be available to talk to the Local 13 Morning Crew about what's going down. Get here in the next ten minutes, and they'll speak with you instead."

"*Fucker.*" I cut myself off, hanging up on him.

running for it

Irritation pulsed in my skull, as I abandoned the idea of coffee, grabbed my purse, and walked out the door. Ramsey had a point that people pulled together for an in-their-face cause, but he'd backed me into a corner. He knew I hated this kind of shit—preening for the camera, pretending to be someone I wasn't— and he'd manipulated me into it regardless.

Fury and frustration poured through me, as I drove to the shelter. I told my phone to send Lyn an apologetic text, saying I was going to be late, I was super sorry, and I'd explain when I got in.

Hopefully, voice recognition sent the right note. With my luck the last few days, it told her I was running away to Aruba, and to fuck off.

True, that didn't sound anything like what I'd said, but who knew?

When I got to the shelter, it wasn't as bad as I'd feared, though it still wasn't great. A single news van sat out front, and none of the kids were around. The parking lot was full, though, so I had to park across the street. The neighbors must be hating this, and they didn't need another reason to complain about us.

"Violet." Hunter's call drew my attention. He was on the other street-facing side of the main building, waving me over.

The cameraman, reporter, and Ramsey weren't too far from him.

"There she is." The reporter was a large Hawaiian man who called himself Kool Kahuna for the cameras. He and Ramsey approached me, wearing twin grins, while the camera stayed behind. "Pleasure to meet you." Kahuna shook my hand vigorously.

"Same. I'm a huge fan." It was true. I'd learned to hide *star struck* when I was dating Ramsey. The after-parties he got us into at Sundance helped a lot with that. But Kahuna was a friendly, cheerful presence on TV, and rumor was he was just as kind in real life.

"We only have a few minutes until we're live again, so if you want to join us, we need to make this quick," Kahuna said. "You ever do live TV before?"

I shook my head. "But I'm not bad at beating stage fright."

He nudged Ramsey. "You spend any time with this guy, and that's a given. Am I right? So this is a little different, since it's live. There are no retakes. No do-overs. But it doesn't matter. We'll have fun with any flubs, and I make them all the time. You stall for any reason, nudge my foot, and I'll step in. Ramsey asked me not to mention that this was a GLBT shelter, so we're only calling it a youth shelter. I'm going to ask you basic questions about what you do here. Keep names out of it. Any questions?"

running for it

"I don't think so." I was still processing the current information, and my missed coffee that was so far away. I was grateful they were keeping the full nature of the shelter out of things, not because I was embarrassed, but because the last thing these kids needed was some new hate group showing up on their lawn, protesting their existence.

"Great. Producer says we're on in sixty. Love the look by the way. *Down to earth* is perfect. Lighting's best on this side of the house. Let's go." He jerked his thumb back toward the camera.

Ramsey stepped up beside me as we walked and dipped his head near my ear. "You look amazing, by the way, and I'm glad you made it."

I was still pissed at him, and he hadn't earned the privilege of a response.

The next two hours passed in a blur. Kahuna made it easy to forget the camera was there, and I didn't have to fake any of my answers. All of his questions were focused around getting me to talk about what a great place this shelter was—what a good opportunity it was for the youth.

We had about fifteen minutes between each shoot, and we used it to relocate to different parts of the shelter and make sure we were cleared for filming. At the end of each segment, Kahuna would give the same spiel about the shelter being threatened and looking at relocating, and provide a website address where people could donate if they wanted to help.

A little voice in the back of my mind pointed out Ramsey never once mentioned his campaign. He was there as support and another person to bounce conversation off. It was true Kahuna introduced us both by name each time, but he gave no other context.

When it was all over, I was exhausted, but in a good way. I thanked Kahuna and his staff profusely as they packed up, and then the shelter was quiet.

I still had to deal with Ramsey. Maybe I could just go to work and pretend he wasn't here.

He stepped in front of me, charming-as-fuck smile in place. "Before you yell at me—"

"I'm too worn out to yell," I said. "You already know what I'm going to say."

"Okay, then before you walk out, there's a Part Two to this plan."

We were going to do this after all. "The plan you promised we'd make together? The one you dumped on me out of nowhere anyway? This could have gone so much worse."

"But it didn't."

I clenched my jaw and stared at him. What was I supposed to say that I hadn't delved into a dozen times with him before?

running for it

"I'm sorry." Ramsey's expression softened, and so did his tone. "The producer is a friend. He called me early this morning, said their scheduled show cancelled, and asked if I wanted to do an around-the-town kind of piece for my campaign. I immediately thought of you and the kind of positive exposure this would be for the shelter. I had to give him an answer right away."

It was a reasonable explanation, except— "And then you manipulated me to get me down here."

"I couldn't have you shut this down. Wouldn't you have?"

Probably. And it would have been a mistake. "This wasn't the right way to get this done. You should have given me the chance to decide for myself. Did you see I went along with things when it came down to it? Even without you pulling my strings?"

"Yes, and I'm sorry."

"Don't." I spat. "Don't apologize if you don't mean it."

Chapter Seven

He reached for my hand, and I stepped away from his touch. He frowned. "I do mean it. I should have told you the entire story from the start. I did what felt right at the time, and I see now it wasn't."

I shook my head. *Easier to ask forgiveness than permission.* Such bullshit. Just not usually Ramsey's form of bullshit. If he did something, it was because he knew he was right, no regrets.

"What did you want to tell me?" I shouldn't hear him out, but I was shutting down my heart, so it didn't matter. He'd talk, I'd say *no*, and I'd go to work.

"Part Two. I can make it happen now, but I didn't want to pull the trigger before talking to you."

I narrowed my gaze. "That's what you were going to tell me before I yelled at you?"

"You didn't technically yell," Hunter said. "And we came up with this while we were waiting for the cameras to show up."

"*Hunter* came up with it. But he's right." Was that pride in Ramsey's voice?

running for it

I checked the clock on my phone. "Five minutes? I promised Lyn I'd still be in this morning."

Ramsey rolled his eyes. "She'd let you take the day off. She wouldn't even ask questions."

But I'd hate letting her down. I twisted my mouth, waiting.

"I'll give Dottie a call," Ramsey said. "We'll do a fundraiser in Vegas. Like a pop-up event. Tomorrow night it's there, and at midnight, *poof*— it's gone."

Ramsey's grandmother insisted we call her Dottie, rather than *Dorothy* or *Mrs. Miller*. And she'd done a lot of charity work, and her events made the one last night look like a children's party.

I adored her. She'd reached that age where she was willing to say *fuck it* to what anyone thought, and do things her way. However— "You can't put an entire event together in a day."

Ramsey grinned at the challenge. "Day and a half. I'll call her right now, if you say *yes*. She'd love to do this for you. I'll have the plans for your approval by tonight, and we'll fly out there tomorrow afternoon."

"I can't…" My protest died in my throat, as my gaze landed on the faces pressed to the windows, watching us. I didn't have a choice.

"You're not giving up control; you're delegating. Everything gets your sign-off, down to the caterers and brand of shrimp, if you want." Ramsey knew me too well.

I had a week to find these kids a new place to go, and no funds for it. "All right. Let's do it."

"Perfect." Hunter clapped.

It was adorable.

Ramsey's grin was more assured. "Dinner tonight, as an apology and to discuss strategy?"

"Is this a dinner for the press?" I couldn't help the question. He might not have used this morning to campaign, but now he was donating his valuable time to youth in need. Perfect photo op. I hated that I had to consider the possibility before I gave my answer.

His pleased smugness vanished in a blink. "This is dinner for us."

"No. I can't do this again." I'd almost prefer this were a press dinner. Then Ramsey would be on his best behavior, and I'd see Media Ramsey in action rather than Alpha-Sweet, Sometimes-Nerdy Ramsey.

"It's dinner with friends." Hunter chimed in. "I'll be there too.

He was *so* not a deterrent.

"You have to eat, we have to eat..." Ramsey dangled the thought like the reasonable and honest proposal it was.

That didn't mean I had to eat with them. I did need to approve those plans for tomorrow night,

running for it

though. "Okay. It's a work dinner. We discuss the event tomorrow."

Ramsey raised an eyebrow. "We'll pick you up at six. Get you home before it's too late, because I assume you'll work tomorrow, even though you're about to host a massive fundraiser in another state."

"You assume correctly."

Ramsey stepped closer, and I backed away again.

"I'll see you tonight." I tried not to look too awkward, waving. I wouldn't hold up to a drawn-out *goodbye* and who knew what else. There was no telling what I'd agree to next, especially with my body whispering, *One little farewell kiss wouldn't hurt.*

Lyn's café—Loading Java—was only a few miles from the shelter, and even in morning traffic, I was there in under ten minutes. I rushed inside, past our standard line of early customers, and into the kitchen, where Lyn was grabbing a fresh round of pastries.

Thankfully, she was alone. I'd walked in on her with one of her guys a few times, and while I'm pretty sure she was more embarrassed than me, I wasn't in the mood for unexpected smooches this morning. From anyone.

"I'm so sorry." I grabbed my apron from its hook and tied it in place. "I'll help with morning rush, and then I'll explain." And ask for a day or two off, out of the blue. The idea of dumping that kind of surprise on someone curdled my gut. I'd be letting Lyn down. I *hated* that. Maybe I could miss the party.

But then I was letting someone else beg for money on my shelter's behalf, and I couldn't do that, either.

"Don't worry about it." Lyn was kind. "You looked good this morning. We had it on in here."

Heat flooded my cheeks. "Thanks."

We made it through the morning rush with the practiced efficiency of our well-matched crew. When we hit a lull that looked like it would last at least a few minutes, I pulled Lyn aside.

I explained to her what happened last night with the inspection. And what Ramsey's plan was. "So I may need to take off early tomorrow, and take the day after as well," I said. "I'm *so* sorry. I wish I could give you more warning. I'll ask if anyone can take my shift—"

"It's okay." Lyn sounded like she meant it. "You're doing something important, to you and for others."

I still felt guilty. "But—"

"I get it. Learning to relax and take time off gets easier with each day you take off, though."

I didn't want it to get easier. "I never want to feel right letting people down."

running for it

"You're not letting me down. And don't worry about covering your shift. Owen will do it."

"Okay. Thank you." I was out of arguments.

"If you need anything besides a pop-up Vegas party, let me know," Lyn said. "I have *connections* too. Mine are just less public."

I smiled at the offer. Lyn's friends had helped her remodel this building. I was happy to put them on the payroll to help with mine, as well. "Ask them to be on standby. Whatever comes out of this, I'm going to need a lot of help."

I went back to work, but I couldn't stop thinking about tomorrow. And tonight. Every time *dinner with Ramsey* popped into my head, a giddy little beat danced behind my ribs. It was foolish, but knowing that didn't stop my heart from hoping otherwise.

I spent far too much mental energy on *what should I wear tonight*, as the hours at work ticked away. Especially since when I got home, I didn't know.

My apartment was a simple one-bedroom, with sparse decoration. It suited my needs, and I rarely was here long enough to do more than sleep and shower.

The little black dress in the back of my closet called to me, and I tried to ignore its siren song. I'd bought it because *every girl should have at least one*, and I needed to replace the half-dozen I'd had that reminded me of Ramsey.

The new one hadn't done what I wanted it to. I was wearing a black leather mini when I met Ramsey, and that night, as well as the many others we were together, he could do a whole lot to me when I was in a little black dress, and no one around us was ever the wiser.

Need pulsed between my legs at the rush of memories, and I squeezed my thighs together. Little black dress? Bad idea.

Which must explain why I tugged it from my closet, pulled it on, and accented it with matching heels and thigh-high stockings. At some point, I'd have to admit to myself I wanted this. Wanted him. That having him around in more than a passing-hello way made my pulse skip rope, and I was okay with it.

Being honest about that didn't change the nagging voice, asking me, *What happens when he forces me to choose between him and how we act in public again?*

He'd apologized and I'd avoided him since because I knew spending time with him would break my resolve.

I pinched the bridge of my nose, to stem the flow of conflicting thoughts. It didn't work.

The doorbell ringing did the trick, though.

I grabbed my purse, gave myself one last glance in the mirror, and tried to pretend I wasn't hurrying to answer the door. The way Ramsey looked me over,

running for it

eyes wide and lips pursed in a silent whistle, didn't erase my frown. He and Hunter were dressed casually, in T-shirts and jeans. Though Ramsey's look was more expensive than my dress.

"Ah. It's that kind of night." I forced a chuckle. "Give me five, so I can change."

"Don't you dare." Ramsey grabbed my wrist before I could turn away, his rough grip sending a fresh wave of desire through me.

I sucked in a sharp breath through my teeth, and gestured down with my free hand. "I'm not—"

"You're fine. Better than fine. *Fuck.*" Ramsey finished with a low hiss.

At least the dress had the desired effect. I handed Hunter his freshly washed clothes. "Thank you for these."

He handed the shirt back. "Pull this on."

"It doesn't really match."

"It's perfect. Trust me." His smile was more friendly than hungry, setting an odd contrast of tone. He jerked his thumb behind him. "You'll see the rest outside. Come on."

I pulled on his T-shirt, feeling silly as it hung down almost as far as my dress. I trusted him, though.

We headed down to the parking lot, where Ramsey's Cheyenne waited in a visitor spot. Not that I'd ever seen it before, but it was the most ostentatious-but-practical-for-the-weather thing here.

The locks clicked off with a flash of lights, and Hunter headed for the back of the vehicle. He emerged after only a few seconds, holding two suit coats and ties.

That was so familiar, it muted my muddled emotions around Ramsey and my dress. Both men slipping on the ties over their T-shirts, then shrugging into the jackets was less expected, but it did even things out with my modified outfit.

Ramsey held the front passenger door for me, and grasped my fingers for balance as I stepped up in the seat. Hunter passed me a tablet between the seats, from the spot he'd settled into behind me. There was a bullet-point list on the screen that had to be his.

"This is what Dottie has planned for tomorrow. If she needs a decision from you, it says so. If you have veto power, it says that too. Some things had to be set in stone from the start, like location, so I apologize you don't have 100% control." Hunter leaned in to indicate specific list items. With him this close, his aftershave teased me, and softer memories flitted in my thoughts. Of great conversation. Of curling up next to him and falling asleep. Of so many things.

What was wrong with me?

Chapter Eight

As Ramsey drove and offered running commentary, Hunter went down the party list with me.

"It all looks good." I handed the tablet back. "I'm struggling with the whole gala-overnight thing. Will this really work?"

Hunter huffed a laugh. "Of course. Think of the viral potential. You get a message that says *Pop-up Party in Vegas, to Support LGBTQ+ Youth.* You know that the biggest and best will be at the Luxor, and like Cinderella, it all turns back into a pumpkin at midnight. You want people to know you were there."

Well, *I* didn't care if people knew I was there—not for the reasons he meant—but I got the point. If word got out, if we drew a quarter of the expected donations, I could fix up the shelter. I didn't know what I'd do with the kids while repairs were taking place, but I was working on that. I twisted in my seat, to look at Hunter. "I love it. Thank you."

"Anything for Ramsey's favorite lady." His smile warmed me to my core, but something about his words made my brain stutter.

I couldn't grasp the thought, so I let it go for now.

A short while later, we pulled into a strip-mall parking lot and picked a space in front of a local diner that specialized in ice cream. If you weren't happy with that, they had burgers as well.

"Classy," I teased. "Perfect." The three of us came here all the time in college. Even though Hunter went to a different school, he was Ramsey's roommate then, and hung out with us even outside the bedroom. I'd never minded, because he respected our alone time, and I liked Hunter.

The only other diners inside were a single family, who looked to be finishing up their meal. It was a Monday night in the middle of winter—not a lot of call for ice cream.

The waitress gave us a lingering glance and smirked when she arrived at our table. "Love the outfits." She was sincere. "You know what you're having?"

Same things we always had. Ice cream on a brownie for Ramsey—extra cherries on top. Two scoops of whatever caught my fancy in a waffle cone, and a banana split for Hunter.

running for it

As she left, a new thought occurred to me that I was surprised hadn't before. "This is a formal affair tomorrow night? Or will I show up in my blue satin to everyone dressed in parachute pants and leg warmers, like it's the 80's?"

"That's an oddly specific visual," Hunter said. "And not at all what we planned. There's still time to change things if you'd like."

"Definitely not." I didn't have time to shop, but I had the formal wear on standby.

"Let me take care of the dress. Don't pack anything but toiletries."

I stared blankly at Ramsey, trying to convey, *Do you even know me?* with a gaze. "Like I'm not going to pack for any possibility. Is this so you can make sure I look appropriate?"

"You always look appropriate." His assurance was smooth. "But I want to surprise you."

I frowned. I hated surprises.

"I know. But this one will be good. I promise," Ramsey said.

An awkward lull settled between us. It was worse because we'd never had trouble with conversation in the past. Even the silent moments always felt right. The family on the other side of the dining room left, giving us the entire place to ourselves. Our ice cream arrived, and we dug in, while I tried and failed to ignore the glances Hunter and Ramsey kept exchanging.

This was too much. "How's the campaign going?"

They both looked surprised at the question.

"You really want to talk politics over ice cream?" Hunter asked.

There was no reason. I already had a good idea of what their politics were. "I'm looking for more of a *how are you feeling about the race* kind of vibe."

"I'm set to win the primary." Ramsey's confidence was no surprise.

"Big plans for when you win the general election?" I was pushing him in a specific direction. He'd been groomed by his family for this path. Known for years that he'd do this. So we used to play a game that took things to the extreme.

"Equality." Hunter ticked off one finger. "Prison reform. Schools."

I didn't want a list of public talking points. "This is me. You can give me the *real* dish. No matter how over the top it is." I wanted more fantasy—the *whatever his heart desires* kind not the *tie me up and fuck me* kind. Though…

I shook the second notion away but couldn't get rid of the rush of heat it brought with it. The point of this game was to pick *anything*, no matter how ridiculous. Comic-book-level stuff. Better.

running for it

"Ah." Recognition flashed in Hunter's eyes. He nudged Ramsey. "She wants to know how you're going to *Batman* the place, Bruce Wayne."

Ramsey rolled his eyes. "Don't joke. You know how I feel about Batman."

We did. "That Christian Bale was the pinnacle—"

Hunter joined in. "And no else could ever reach that bar," he said in unison with me. We finished with giggles.

"Don't knock the Dark Knight." Ramsey looked stoic. "He's always watching. Knows when you're sleeping. When you're awake."

Hunter looked like he was struggling to keep a straight face. "That's Santa."

"Who hurt you, that you can't tell the two apart?" I asked with mock concern.

Ramsey stuck his tongue out. "You have to get a lot more naked if you want the illicit details of how I feel about pain."

The heat was back, setting fire to my skin and lighting up my imagination. I had to get back to the fun conversation, so I could get rid of the phantom sensation of Ramsey's palm—his belt, my hair brush—smacking into my ass.

I held my spoon toward Ramsey, using it like a microphone. "So, Councilman Miller, if—*when*—

you're elected, what are your plans for cleaning up crime in the city?"

"Giant robots." There was no hesitation in his response.

I wasn't at all surprised, and I knew where he was going with the answer, but that didn't stop a giggle from slipping out. "As in *Robocop*? *Terminator*? You know Skynet destroyed humanity. While that's technically a crime deterrent, I don't think it's what your constituents are looking for."

"Vibrators and toasters are three percent of the voting population, and all voices deserve to be heard." Hunter rambled off the fake statistic with complete seriousness.

Ramsey cleared his throat and adopted a serious look. "You're not thinking big enough. *Giant* robots. As in, the Grandaddy Gundam, RX-78."

I adored this side of them. The geeky, fanboy side that they didn't show anyone. "Don't mechs tend to destroy cities, Councilman?" I asked.

"Well, actually"—Hunter adopted his best *I'm on the internet and an expert* voice—"you'd find the damage was far worse if you let the monsters roam free. The mechs keep more of the city from being destroyed, even if they themselves are complicit in the destruction."

I laughed and shook my head in disbelief. "Spoken like a true politician. I'm not sure the threats

running for it

to Salt Lake are Neon Zeos." I said the name wrong on purpose, with a lilt of teasing in my voice.

Ramsey clenched his jaw.

I stared at him, eyes wide and innocent. "Is something wrong, Councilman?"

"It's Neo Zeongs. And you know that."

Another laugh slipped out. Goddess, this was familiar and good in the best possible way, and I was way past wanting it not to. "Maybe."

"You're such a brat, Taffy."

I shrugged in agreement. "What are you going to do? Bend me over your knee and spank me?"

"Aww." Hunter pouted. "I want to be spanked."

My brain slid to a halt.

Ramsey placed a finger under Hunter's chin and raised his head to meet his gaze. "Of course. She hasn't earned it. You just have to beg."

Heat spilled through me, and I struggled to catch up. Not only was the exchange flat-out adorably sexy, it was also anything but friendly. Yesterday morning, ungodly early, replayed in my brain. Me, waking up, still hazy, to find Ramsey saying, *I'll talk to you in a few hours*, and giving Hunter a *goodbye* kiss...

Fuck me. I was such a blind idiot. "You two are together." The words came out louder than I intended. Ramsey glared at me and I clapped my hands over my mouth. A glance around us said no one was paying attention to the silly friends in the corner booth.

My heart dropped into my shoes. I was letting myself fall into a *what if* fantasy with Ramsey, and he was in a relationship. I was a side dish. Not even what Hunter had been to us in the past, because he was a friend. I was just the ex.

"You didn't think to mention this—I don't know—two days ago?" Before I climbed back into bed with them. Before I stood on the edge of the *delusion* rabbit hole and considered jumping in, headfirst?

They exchanged a look, and Ramsey gave a slight shake of his head.

Hunter turned back to me. "We don't tell anyone, which you probably noticed."

"You just made sure everyone saw you at one fundraiser helping kids like you, and you're fast-laning another, and you feel like you have to hide who you are?" I wasn't accusing them; I was genuinely curious.

Ramsey sighed. "There's a difference between supporting a cause and being the cause. You know that. If I came out, the focus would be on my gayness—because you know I wouldn't be bisexual to the media—and not what others needed."

That was surprisingly altruistic and painfully realistic. "Imagine the kind of role model you'd be."

running for it

"An amazing one," Ramsey said. "But I'm not the only one I'm thinking about." He looked at Hunter. "Maybe someday I'll—*we'll*—get there, but not yet. I'm a rich white boy, who's played straight my entire life. Letting my money and other, more experienced individuals speak is more helpful."

I wanted to argue that this was another version of his public face versus his private one, but I understood not outing people before they were ready. For all the acceptance out there, just as much bigotry still existed. And it was sweet that he was worried about Hunter in that way.

Hunter tugged one of my fingers, drawing my attention. "What happened after the party? We don't make a habit of that."

"God, no." Ramsey shook his head.

Of course they didn't. "Because it would look bad if it got out."

Hunter raised an eyebrow. "Because that's not the lifestyle either of us wants. I don't care if other people open their relationships, but I'm selfish with my guy."

My guy. So much possession in the simple phrase. And my jealousy was skyrocketing. Then again, they hid what they had, and I'd always made it clear I wasn't interested in being someone different in the bedroom than I was out of it. They hid their relationship so well, I felt bad for Hunter. I'd hated having to fake-smile when I was with Ramsey, and he had to fake-everything.

I shut off all my *what happens next* fantasies about Ramsey. "Thank you for the ice cream. It was fun hanging out again. See you tomorrow?"

"You're taking this wrong." Hunter settled a hand on my bare knee, startling me.

"What happened after the party wasn't a mistake." Ramsey tangled his fingers with mine. "It's not what we planned, but there are no regrets. You're not just a warm body."

Hunter squeezed my knee. "You're Violet."

"I don't know what that means." But I wanted to, so desperately, just based on the pair of simple touches.

Chapter Nine

Ramsey dropped a large bill on the table and tugged both Hunter and me to our feet. "You wanted to go home. Let's get out of here."

"I *want* to finish this conversation." I reluctantly pulled my hand away and crossed my arms, mostly to keep temptation at bay.

Ramsey held my gaze, never letting go of Hunter. "So do I."

I tapped my toes inside my shoes, as my brain followed a series of possible outcomes based on hope, experience, and cynicism. I couldn't argue that this was a private conversation, but there was no one here to eavesdrop, unless the staff got bored with their gossip about their co-workers. Having this conversation in the car meant I couldn't look them in the eye while we talked, and I needed that. Going to someone's house meant the temptation of clothes coming off, given the topic, or disappointment I shouldn't feel if the clothes stayed on.

"Talk to me now," I said.

Ramsey sighed and raked his fingers through his hair. "This is not the way I wanted things to go."

"Sorry you can't control every single little bit of life."

He raised an eyebrow. "You talking to me or yourself?"

I opened my mouth to retort, and he held up a finger. "I'm not trying to pick a fight," Ramsey said. "Sit back down, at least?"

"Fine." It was a reasonable request, given I was refusing to leave without answers. We took our spots around the table again.

Ramsey leaned in, but there was no contact. "You know I miss you. I've never hidden that."

And yet, you're with someone else. I swallowed the retort. Did I expect him to wait for me, when I'd made it clear we weren't happening? Especially if he had a chance with Hunter?

"Two nights ago was amazing," Ramsey said. "We had a long talk after." He indicated Hunter. "You and I are good together, Taffy. We need to try again."

And I was the idiot who wanted to. Fortunately, I didn't have to decide. "Hunter said he didn't want an open relationship."

"I don't. This isn't open. It's for you alone, and we'll talk about what that means if you're interested," Hunter said.

running for it

Exclusive offer. Limited time only. Step inside for details. I stifled a barking laugh at the rush of random thoughts and stood again. "I can't…" Couldn't what? Give him a part of me again. As much as I ached to pursue this topic. "I'm gonna catch a bus home. I'll see you tomorrow." Fuck. I had to see them tomorrow.

I needed to make sense of my thoughts before I could look them in the eye. The jumbled mess in my brain wouldn't do at all.

I strode toward the door.

"Violet." Ramsey's call hit my back, as I stepped outside.

The cold blast stung against my hot cheeks, but I didn't pause.

"Violet." Ramsey had caught up to me now, his voice near enough he didn't have to shout.

I still couldn't look.

He grabbed my arm as we passed his SUV, and he spun my back to the vehicle so I faced him. We stared each other down, as my desire warred with fury over how he'd restrained me. I swore sparks raced between us. I could step closer, but I'd be hard pressed to move away, the way he had me boxed in.

Ramsey let go of me and moved away a few paces. "Don't take the bus." His voice was flat. "Let me drive you home."

I'll be fine. "All right. Thank you." I climbed into the back seat before he could offer another option. Hunter was his boyfriend. They should be sitting next to each other.

No one said anything, as Ramsey pulled onto the main road. With as little production as possible, I took off Hunter's shirt, folded it, and handed it to him.

"Thanks." His voice was impossible to read.

This wasn't what I wanted. I wasn't upset at either of them. Maybe I should be about the way they'd hidden their relationship—I would have liked to know that before I climbed into bed with them—but in a certain light, I understood.

So what was my problem? Why couldn't I talk to them or even look at them?

Because I *did* still want something more with Ramsey, and my reasons for leaving him hadn't changed. I was immensely jealous of Hunter. Was this what it had been like for him? Occasionally being invited into our bed? Having to watch from the outside, the rest of the time?

There are no regrets about what happened. Ramsey's words snuck into my thoughts.

I didn't regret it either. I wanted more of it. If I had them drop me off tonight, and kept this conversation closed, would I regret that?

running for it

"What you're talking about…" My voice came out wobblier than I wanted, and I licked my lips. I hadn't wanted to do this without being able to look them in the eye, but I'd rather that than not doing it at all. "It's not like what Lyn has with Kingston and Owen."

The three of them loved each other. They were happily exclusive. Hunter was a friend, but he wasn't more, even if it was tempting to think of him as the competition.

"I don't know what it is," Ramsey said. "I want to see you again—date you, before you tell me I can already see you. I'm not going to ask that you don't see anyone else, even if I want to. That's not fair of me, because I'm not giving up Hunter."

It sounded straightforward. Could I do it? I was more torn on the letting-Ramsey-back-into-my-life thing than I was about sharing him with Hunter. "It doesn't erase the problems we had before."

"We'll work through those," Ramsey said quickly.

I fiddled with the hem of my dress. The short, flared skirt I'd worn specifically for him. I tapped Hunter on the shoulder. "And you're okay with this?"

"I already have the guy. Hard to argue with the position I'm in." He glanced back at me.

Fuck it. "All right. Let's give it a try."

We pulled into my apartment parking lot, and Ramsey opened the back driver's side door for me. As I swung my legs to the side, to climb out, he moved in, pinning my wrist to the seat. He slid between my legs, the fabric of his trousers teasing my thighs.

He licked a slow line up my neck, to my ear. "Tell me you didn't wear this dress for me."

"I did." My anticipation was back, whimpering for more. It was different, knowing Hunter sat in the front seat, where he could watch but it wouldn't be easy for him to participate. What did he think of this?

Ramsey let go of one of my wrists, to move his hand under my skirt. He teased the elastic of my underwear. "And yet, you wore panties."

"Never stopped you before."

"And it won't stop me now." Ramsey glided his finger along my skin then lower over the lace. He stroked along the crotch, pressing enough to tease, and drew his mouth to mine, claiming my lips in a series of hungry pecks.

"What about Hunter?" I asked between kisses.

"I rarely mind a good show." His voice from behind me was husky. "And I always enjoy you two."

A good show. We were in the visitor parking of an apartment complex, half hanging out of an SUV, and anyone could walk by. The thrill of

running for it

getting caught, putting on a show for a random stranger, made my pulse race. But, "Are you worried about being seen. You being you?" It never stopped Ramsey before, but who knew now?

"No." His reply was hot against my neck. He shoved my panties aside and slipped his fingers to my clit. "I'm not whipping out my dick, just giving my date a goodnight kiss." He teased lightly.

"While your fingers wander," I managed between gasps.

He dipped lower, gliding inside me to thrust over and over. "Exactly."

My hips swayed to his touch. My breath came in short pants. We might not be visible to most people, but Hunter knew exactly what we were doing. That made me clench with need.

Ramsey withdrew his fingers and moved back to my clit, stroking hard this time. Drawing tiny circles. Pressing and teasing and nudging me to teeter on the edge of climax.

"Come for me, Taffy," he growled into my neck.

My laugh was shaky. "I don't do that on demand. That's not how this works."

"No?" Ramsey worked faster. "What if I tell you once you're inside tonight, I'm going back to Hunter's." He pushed me closer. Orgasm was just out of reach. "I'm going to fuck the hell out of him, while this moment is still fresh in our minds."

Yeah, that was pretty fucking hot. I bit the inside of my cheek to keep from crying out as Ramsey's words and touch sent me topping into ecstasy. Every inch of me shuddered with the release of desire, and I ground into his touch until I was spent, and my body shuddered away.

I rested my hands on the seat behind me to keep myself upright.

Ramsey pressed two slick fingers to my lips and I drew them in, greedily sucking myself from his skin. He kissed me around the touch. Around the licking. Sharing my flavor. His tongue dancing with mine and around his fingers.

We finally broke the kiss and he rested his forehead against mine. "I wish I could take you home with us tonight. I can, can't I?"

I wanted to. So desperately. "I have to work in the morning, and I won't get any sleep if I go with you."

"No, you really won't." He pulled away with one more kiss. "At least let me walk you to your door."

I couldn't argue that request, and I really couldn't ignore how badly it sucked to stay here after they left.

running for it

Only a few days back in my life, and I was already completely smitten with Ramsey again. I was so fucked. In more ways than one.

Chapter Ten

I was always grateful I'd been born with the *multi-task like a boss* gene, but this morning, more than ever. As I worked through my routine at Loading Java, a portion of my mind was focused on last night. The conversation with Ramsey. What we agreed to. What came after.

Those thoughts wouldn't be dissuaded.

In the midst of all that, I made a series of calls to local extended-stay motels. Whether the shelter moved to a new building or was just remodeled, the kids would need someplace to stay in the interim. This was the best temporary solution I could come up with. A couple of the volunteers would be on hand at all times, like they were now, and we'd make the situation work.

I breathed a sigh of relief when I found a motel willing to reserve an entire floor for us for the next two weeks. It was a great starting point.

The hours both sped by and crawled at a snail's pace. I was in the back room, doing inventory on teacups, when I heard a voice boom from out front.

running for it

"I'd like to speak to the manager. Now." Hunter's tone wasn't nearly as threatening as the words implied it should be.

A silly grin bounced onto my face, and I didn't try to stop it as I stepped into the shop. "What can I do for you, sir?" Besides question why he was alone.

"How much for… you?"

I was surprised he asked that in front of customers and other employees. Then again, he wasn't Ramsey. I clucked. "You can't afford me."

"I'll buy you lunch."

I screwed my face up, pretending to consider the offer. "In Las Vegas?"

"Sold." He grinned. "You ready to go?"

"Thirty seconds." I ducked into the kitchen, to grab my purse and duffel bag. It didn't matter that Ramsey told me not to pack anything; I still had a few changes of clothes and an emergency dress, just in case. I joined Hunter, and we made our way out to his car.

"Ramsey's sorry he's not here himself," Hunter said as he held the passenger door for me. "He's stuck in a meeting. He'll meet us at the airport."

I understood that. It was disappointing to not see him now, but I would soon enough. "No big deal."

Hunter took his place behind the wheel, and we were on our way.

"I'm curious," I said. "What does a campaign manager do?"

He navigated lunchtime traffic downtown like a pro. "You manage Lyn's place. What do you do?'

"Inventory. Scheduling. Opening and closing the shop. Anything Lyn tells me to."

"There you have it."

We both knew the work wasn't that basic. "Anything Ramsey tells you to? Is this a paid position? Volunteer? Do you get paid to be his boyfriend?"

Hunter shot me a half-dry, half-amused look. "Volunteer. Never question that I serve him for free." There was a hint of teasing in his voice.

"That's fair. And don't give me a glossed-over answer like that. You know I need details."

"Something I adore about you." He merged onto the freeway. "But details always depend on the situation. I make sure all the parts are clicking *behind* the scenes, so he can focus on *the scenes*. I do the hiring. Scheduling. Inventory—banners, buttons, shirts. Whatever he needs that he's not thinking of, because he's focused on other priorities."

Impressive. I let out an exaggerated *that's so sweet* sigh. "So dreamy. I know most people think details are boring, but the way you talk about them is so sexy."

running for it

He tapped me lightly on the nose. "You don't have to win me over. I'm already there."

"I wasn't even thinking about that. I'm serious. I like a guy who has a grasp of how many *Miller for Senate* T-shirts are in the back room."

"I can't tell you that off the top of my head or anything."

"Uh-huh." I let the disbelief drip from my retort.

Hunter sighed heavily. "Seventeen small, thirteen medium, thirteen large, and two XL's. New shipment will be in Thursday."

"See?" I asked playfully.

Hunter shook his head, but he was smiling as we pulled into the airport. He opened his mouth, and his phone rang, cutting him off. "You okay if I take this?"

"Of course."

I listened to Hunter's half of administrative details. I'd meant what I said—most people would find this boring, but I adored how on top of things he was.

As he talked, he turned the car toward a part of the airport I wasn't familiar with, and parked us in an empty lot.

Security was nothing like I was used to. We were in and out in just a few minutes, and walking out the gate, to climb a short set of stairs to a small jet.

I stalled in the plane's doorway. I'd never seen something like this in person—it was straight out of the movies, with the leather and wood and so much space for an airplane. Yeah, Ramsey and I had traveled a few times when we dated, and I thought First Class was opulent. But this was the family jet, and he hadn't had access to it back then.

I guess he'd *earned it*.

"Hey." Ramsey's greeting jarred me from my awe. "Sorry I had to meet you here."

Hunter stepped around me. "'S'all good."

"Totally fine," I said. Sometimes work demanded a little extra time and responsibility.

"Hey, handsome." Ramsey tugged Hunter in for a long, heated kiss.

That he reached for Hunter first stung, but *Goddess* was it amazing to watch.

Ramsey let Hunter go, and turned to me. "I'm glad you're here." His voice was low and smooth. He brushed his lips over mine, lightly enough to tempt and tease, then deepened the kiss. Desire sang over and through me, all the way to my core.

I'd missed this feeling so much.

Ramsey stepped back. "Lady and Gentleman, take your seats. Let's go to Vegas."

running for it

I settled into a spot that was more comfortable than my living-room furniture. This would be a short flight, so there was no reason to take advantage of the amenities. However, it was tempting to at least see what kind of secrets a plane like this held.

As we taxied toward the runway, my phone rang. "Sorry. I forgot to turn it off."

"Go ahead and take it." Ramsey waved a hand. "No restrictions here."

Talk about decadent. "Hello?"

"Is this Violet?" the woman on the other end of the line asked.

"It is."

"This is Tawna, from Extended Stop Motels. We talked earlier?" Her voice was timid, which it hadn't been earlier.

"Of course. What can I do for you?"

"I got a call from corporate, and they had me cancel your reservation."

Disappointment sank into my bones. This had been the only place on my list that even talked to me. No one wanted to rent an entire floor to a group of kids. Too much liability. "Did they say why? Is there anything I can do?"

"They said there were insurance issues. Problems with legal guardianship. Liability concerns."

I clenched my jaw and turned away from the two sets of eyes watching me. "Those are just a bunch of phrases. They don't mean anything." They did, but I couldn't let this reservation fall apart.

"I'm sorry." Tawna's voice was tight. "I'm happy to let you stay here, but this came down from corporate. It's out of my hands."

It wouldn't do me any good to yell at her. "I get it. Thank you." I dropped my phone into my lap and scrubbed my face, letting a long breath out through my fingers.

"What's wrong?" Ramsey's question was all concern.

If I left this until tomorrow, would it give me enough time to find a solution? I'd need at least that long, to think of what to try next. "Nothing. I've got it." My hands muffled my words.

"Would you have it faster or less painfully if we helped you brainstorm?" Ramsey asked.

Yes. No. Maybe.

Warm hands grabbed my wrists, and Ramsey pushed them into my lap as he moved into the seat next to me. "Talk."

"If I don't, will you stop asking?"

"Nope."

As I told them what was going on, it was impossible to hide my frustration. Sometimes,

running for it

talking through something presented answers, but this time, I drew a blank.

Hunter had his phone out. "Give me thirty minutes."

"I can't." I shook my head.

Ramsey squeezed my hand gently. *"Can't* what?"

"Can't keep asking for favors. I owe you both too much."

Hunter stared at me with disbelief.

"That's not the way this works." Was that hurt in Ramsey's voice?

Who was he kidding? "That's exactly the way this works."

Ramsey placed a finger under my chin and turned my face toward his. "This isn't *tit for tat.* We're not keeping score. You're a friend who needs help, and Hunter can help. If one of us needed something, you'd do the same."

"What would you need from me?" I wanted to take back the question as soon as I asked it. Mostly because I hated feeling like I couldn't contribute— and what was I offering them in return, for everything they were doing?

"You know better than that," Hunter said. "If you don't, I'm telling you now. Money and connections get a lot of things done, but not everything, and frequently not the important things."

There was an underlying thread in his voice I couldn't identify.

"So, I've got this." He dialed.

My *thank you* was muffled by his talking to whoever picked up on the other end.

I listened intently to his half of each conversation, trying to tell how things were going. It didn't work. He briefly explained the situation each time, followed by short, pleasant answers, and then he'd hang up.

The fact that he kept making calls made my heart sink. We landed, and he was dialing more people. We were getting in the car, when he *whooped*. "Got it."

The car was big enough that two bench-seats faced each other in back. Ramsey slid in next to me, and Hunter took the spot across from us. Everything about his expression and posture said *pleased*.

"Eight-plex in Sugar House. All of them two-bedroom, two-bath," Hunter said. "The new owner had everyone move out because he's remodeling, but the bank held his financing. The place is empty for at least two months, and your kids can stay there. No charge. He'll write it off as a donation."

"You're the best." I leaned across the divide, to give him a *thank you* hug.

running for it

"I wanna be the best." Ramsey's pouty voice was exaggerated. He wrapped an arm around my waist and yanked me into his lap.

I squirmed more than was needed to get comfortable, feeling him half-harden underneath me. "You are the absolute best."

"Mhm." He scraped his teeth over my neck. "At what?"

"Everything? What are you looking for?" I teased.

Ramsey bit my shoulder hard enough to draw a yelp, sending a spark of desire through me. "Something sincere would be nice," he growled.

"No one hurts me like you do." That sounded bad. "I mean that in the best way possible."

"Mhm," he repeated, settling his hands on my hips and moving me into my own spot.

Had I offended him?

Chapter Eleven

Ramsey leaned in, to hover his lips near my ear, his warm breath teasing my skin. "You need a little pampering, in case there's more agony later," he said in a stage whisper.

"I have no idea what that means." Was it supposed to be sexy? Threatening? I was pretty sure it meant he wasn't offended by my comment.

He chuckled. "I thought it was a clever segue, but maybe not. You have an appointment at the hotel salon in about"—he looked at his empty wrist—"fifteen minutes."

If pressed by the right person, I had to admit I missed this part of dating Ramsey. The part where certain things that I considered luxuries and he considered necessities were paid for by default. I'd have to be pressed hard, though, because even admitting it to myself made me feel selfish. "If you insist."

"I do."

We reached the hotel, and Ramsey gave my hand a quick squeeze and promised they'd see me in

running for it

a few hours, and a member of the staff showed me to my appointment.

The stylist yanked the scrunchie out of my hair with a sigh. "At least it's not elastic. Says in your appointment notes you can do whatever you'd like, as long as you don't cut more than a couple of inches off."

Because of course Ramsey sent instructions. Those weren't as specific as usual, though. "I could have you dye it blue?"

"In the amount of time we have? Yes, if you want to destroy these gorgeous curls."

I didn't. "I trust you. Make me look like a princess, going to a ball. More Meghan Markle than Cinderella," I added as an afterthought.

"You got it, hon."

The next few hours were almost enough to make me forget the looming party, from having my scalp massaged, and my fingers and feet soaked and rubbed. The stunning blue polish… I didn't even have to ask. I hoped the color raised a few eyebrows.

When I handed my personal stylist a tip, she gave me a keycard with a room number.

"I'm told your things are already up there," she said.

"Thank you, for a wonderful experience."

I checked my phone as I took the elevator up. How was it already four? The party didn't start until seven, but I couldn't walk in there—couldn't let guests arrive—without looking everything over first. And now my nervousness was back.

I stepped into the kind of hotel room I thought only existed in movies. The living room was bigger than my entire apartment, with three couches, white carpet, and gold everywhere. A door at the far end led to a bedroom, that I assumed was equally as overwhelming.

Ramsey was waiting, already dressed for the night in his tux. *Goddess*, he was breathtaking.

"You look incredible. And you probably want to get downstairs ridiculously early," he said. "Hunter will meet us there."

"You know me so well. I'm feeling a little underdressed, though." I gestured down.

Ramsey reached for a long bag hanging on the back of a nearby door. "Clothes off."

I raised an eyebrow, and he stared back at me with a look that said, *Argue with me. I dare you.*

It was tempting, but the clock was ticking, and if I pushed back, we'd be here for a while. Oh, and I'd mess up my hair. But the way Ramsey was watching me, with barely hidden desire, I didn't care.

"Can we pretend I argued, and you can punish me later?" I asked sweetly.

He huffed. "I guess."

running for it

I kicked off my shoes, then stripped off my shirt, intently aware of how he watched my every movement. "How much is everything?" I asked.

"Everything is *everything*." Ramsey's tone was hard.

Right. Desire roared over me, as I removed my jeans, my bra, and finally my panties, leaving me naked and on display in the middle of the room.

Ramsey closed the distance between us, stopping far enough away I couldn't feel his heat, but I could reach out and touch him.

Self-consciousness wanted me to cover up, but I fought the impulse.

He dragged a finger along my jaw, down my neck, to my arm, and lower, to grasp my fingers. He kissed the tips. "Love the blue."

My entire body was probably flushed pink, but I didn't dare look.

Ramsey smirked and returned to the dress bag. He unzipped it, to reveal swaths of black underneath. It was a stunning gown. I'd never worn anything so elegant.

He unzipped the dress and beckoned me with a finger, as he removed the dress from its hanger. "Arms up."

"I—" didn't have any panties on.

"Yes?" He watched me with that look of challenge again.

I put my arms up. "Nothing."

Ramsey moved behind me, to slip the dress over my head. He slid his palms down my sides, smoothing out the skirt even though it mostly fell to the floor on its own. He zipped up the back, sucking everything into place. Looking down, I could see the scooped neck, the skirt with a slit almost the hip, and the off-the shoulder short sleeves.

I wanted to see the whole deal from a better angle, though. I stepped toward the three-way mirror, and Ramsey grabbed my arm. "Not yet."

I heard some light shuffling and a faint *click*. The cool touch of metal met my neck, and I looked down to see a strand of diamonds and sapphires that fell to a stop right in the middle of my cleavage. The light danced off the gems in tiny rainbows.

"It's only a loaner." Ramsey trailed his fingers down my spine. When he took his hand away, the weight of another chain rested on my back. "Now you can look."

I moved in front of the mirror and gasped. I really did look like a princess, including the stunning back necklace that was undoubtedly worth more than the sum of my worldly possessions. After a few spins, so I could see myself from every possible angle, Ramsey joined me.

running for it

He rested his hands on my shoulders, just below the sleeves, and pressed into my back. "You're breathtaking."

I really did look incredible. "This sets a new bar in the little-black-dress department."

"I don't mind." Ramsey dragged his lips up my neck, to rest in the hollow behind my ear.

I met his gaze in our reflection. We were straight out of a fairytale.

"The last few days have been a whirlwind, even by our standards." He moved his hands to my hips, holding me tight. "I want to make sure you're still okay with what we talked about last night."

"The dating again, or the fact that we're explicitly non-exclusive?" My non-answer was a stall, and it shouldn't have been. I should have been able to say *absolutely* without hesitation.

"I was thinking the latter, but now that you ask, both."

I frowned. This was when I should move away, but I didn't want to lose his touch. "I want to be okay with it."

"But you're not."

"I don't know. I'm not *not* okay with it. It feels like it's worth seeing through."

Ramsey pressed his lips to my neck again, letting the kiss linger. "I feel it's worth it too. When we get home, we'll have some alone time, just you and me. Catch up. Actually date."

I leaned more of my weight into him. It was a lovely suggestion. "When are you going to have time for all of this? Me. Hunter. Alone. Together. Campaigning."

"When are you?" he countered. "Loading Java. The shelter. You're about to move into either a massive remodel or a construction project…"

Touché. "I'll figure it out."

"Exactly." Ramsey tangled his fingers with mine and pulled us from the mirror. "I almost forgot…" He pulled a shoe box from the dresser.

A pair of stilettos sat inside, with straps that wove in a crisscross over the foot and had ridiculously long leather laces.

He set them on the floor. "I'll tie you up."

"Frequently." I laughed and let him slip on the first shoe. He wove the laces up my calf and tied them a few inches below the knee. With the slit in the dress, only a hint would show when I walked. It was the perfect subtle touch.

Ramsey secured the second shoe and stood. "Those, you can keep. In fact, only the necklace has to be returned tomorrow." He held out his bent arm. "Shall we?"

I hooked my hand near the crook of his elbow. "Let's."

running for it

Our path took us downstairs and out back, to a set of tents. It didn't look very fancy from the outside, but stepping into one was like moving into an entirely different world. I had no idea how they put chandeliers in the middle of a tent. Crystal lined the tables. There was silk and linen everywhere.

"It's stunning." My awe tumbled past my lips.

"Isn't it, thought?" Hunter joined us. He looked me over, brows raised. "Though… no competition. You look incredible."

"Thanks. Ramsey has good taste."

Hunter nodded. "So much truth there. You ready for the grand tour, to set your mind at ease?"

If the main hall looked like this, I wasn't too concerned about how everything else looked, but I did want to see for myself.

For the next hour or so, Hunter led us through to the kitchen and the staging area, and gave us a sample of the hors d'oeuvres.

It was all amazing. I grasped for words but couldn't find them.

"You okay?" Ramsey asked.

"I can't believe you made all of this happen. Because I asked." It was so much.

He settled his hand on the small of my back. "Of course I did. *You* asked. The cause is as important as it gets as well, but…"

I kept my mouth shut, waiting for him to finish the thought.

Hunter leaned in. "But you are and always have been at the center of his universe," he said softly.

Was that envy I heard in Hunter's voice?

"Ah. Violet."

I cringed at the woman's familiar voice, but pasted on a flat expression before I turned to face her. "Debbie." I extended my hand. "Good to actually meet you." For all I knew, she was a nice person, and the other night really had been an honest mistake.

Her grip was too firm, and her hands hot and dry. Her smile looked painted on. "Same. Will we be seeing a lot of you, going forward?"

"Absolutely." Ramsey spoke before I could consider the appropriate answer.

Why wasn't that my default reply?

"Fantastic." Debbie's smile was as fake as the little rhinestones glued to the roots of my nails. She gave all her attention to Ramsey. "I need to borrow you for some photos. I promise to return you intact when I'm done."

"No problem. I'll catch up with you two soon." Ramsey was cool and professional, as he walked away.

That was new. Sure, he wore a mask in public when we dated, but he never shied away from contact. Small affections. Except the equation was

running for it

more complicated now. Did that devour Hunter—having to hide who he was? Who they were? I already didn't like it.

"Debbie seems nice." I couldn't think of anything else to say.

Hunter looked at me with surprise. "Really?"

"Shouldn't she?" So I wasn't the only one she rubbed wrong.

"To each their own. I'm not a fan, but she's the best at her job."

"Being pushy, possessive, and bitchy?" I should have kept the thought to myself, but Hunter wouldn't mind.

He laughed. "Getting people elected. Never doubt for a moment that I'm the queen of possessive and bitchy in Ramsey's life." His tone was light, but it tugged on his comment from earlier, about me.

"I'm not trying to move in on your relationship." There were more people now, so I kept my comment vague.

"I know." Hunter steered me to the edge of the room, away from the staff. "I also know when Ramsey sets his sights on a goal, he doesn't stop until he's met it. His sights have never left you."

Ramsey'd moved on, though. "But you and he..." Weren't just close, they also shared bits of their life I'd never be a part of.

"Yeah." Could Hunter read my mind? Or did he recognize both halves of the equation? "And I believe him when he tells me how he feels about me. But there's always a sliver of envy and resentment."

"For me?"

"I assume the question is rhetorical, but yes."

Hunter's statement gripped me hard. I didn't want to be that stumbling block in someone else's relationship. It made me feel dirty and uncomfortable, and the fact that Hunter had been part of the sex made it worse. Had I been fucked a guy who didn't like me? Who didn't want me around? But he'd assured me it was fine. "You said… about the last two nights… Was that…" A lie for Ramsey's sake?

Chapter Twelve

"Was I being sincere?" Hunter filled in my unfinished question with a very different response. "Absolutely. That's what you wanted to ask, right? Because you don't assume I'd use you."

Not that I was going to admit to now.

Hunter sighed and leaned his weight against the wall. He tugged on my fingertips and held on as our arms hung between us. "Just because I'm jealous you're a permanent part of my boyfriend's life, doesn't mean I don't like you." His voice was almost a whisper. "I'm a complex individual, capable of feeling more than one thing at once."

"Do you want me to not do this?" Awkward phrasing.

He shook his head. "I would have said so, if that were the case."

"But—"

"First of all, backing away from something you want isn't any more *you* than it is *Ramsey*. You're giving it another try because you feel something for him."

"Yes." I almost felt guilty admitting it.

"And second, you're not responsible for how I feel. You can't second-guess anything outside of what I tell you."

I wanted to argue that I could try. That instinct and reading beyond the surface—seeing the subtext—was necessary in their world.

Hunter pushed away from the wall, pulling me with him. "How about this? I enjoy your company. I like the way Ramsey lights up when you're around. All of that outweighs the jealousy. I mean that. You don't have to dig through it for a double meaning. I'd rather have you around than not. But whether you decide to stay with Ramsey—to hang out with me—has to be based on what you want and what we all agree on. Not on what you think one of us might want that we haven't said."

That was a lot to absorb. "You're so fucking reasonable sometimes."

"I'm reasonable all the time. To a fault. Besides"—Hunter leaned in so his mouth was near my ear—"you're the only woman I've ever enjoyed fucking, and *gods*, do I enjoy it."

I smiled past the flush in my veins. "You're such a charmer."

"Junior League Champion, three years running."

running for it

And now we were back to being *us*. I was good with that. The teasing wouldn't silence my inner nagging over his confession, but I appreciated his honesty. "Of charming?"

"Of everything, I assume. I'm the full package, babe."

"You most definitely are."

We chatted until guests started trickling—and then pouring—in. Ramsey still hadn't returned. I recognized a handful of people, but for the most part, this was all new territory. Hunter seemed to know everyone, though. He introduced me to one person after another, always with a one- or two-sentence snippet about them, to help me remember who they were.

"Violet. Hunter." Dottie's familiar call came from behind.

We turned to find Ramsey's grandmother approaching, wearing the warmest smile of anyone in here. She wasn't a frail old granny. She was as tall as Hunter, in her heels, and unlike most of the women here, she wore a tailored suit.

She gave me a quick hug and a kiss on the cheek. "I was so happy to hear your name when Ramsey called me. I've missed you."

"Same." I meant it. I didn't know my grandparents, but Dottie always treated me like a member of the family.

"I'm glad you're here, too." She greeted Hunter with the same hug and kiss. "Where's my Crow?" That was her nickname for Ramsey. She said his parents had missed out by naming one child Ravyn and not naming the other in kind. Especially since, like a crow, Ramsey always insisted on being heard.

Hunter gestured broadly. "Your guess is as good as mine. Publicity photos, I assume."

Dottie raised an eyebrow and looked at me. "Does he realize this is your event, not his?"

"Not his doing." I assured her.

"He's perfectly capable of telling the media hounds *no*." Dottie squeezed my hand. "When you see him, tell him I'm looking for him. And I hope I'll be seeing more of both of you."

A call pulled Dottie away, and Hunter and I were left to mingle again. The shoes Ramsey picked out were amazing, but not for standing in for hours. After I was certain I'd talked to everyone at least twice, I begged off to a quiet corner, to sit for a little bit, with Hunter for company.

That was where Ramsey found us. "Hey." He pulled out another chair across from us, frustration etched on his face. "Debbie set up an interview and didn't tell me first." He looked at Hunter. "Don't worry. I've told her this not-warning-me-first shit doesn't fly."

running for it

But he'd done the interview anyway, because he couldn't turn away the perfect press opportunity. I didn't have to ask if that was the case. The fact that he'd vanished for several hours said it all. I almost wished my brain defaulted to *maybe he was* with *someone*. It wasn't a concern, though, even before he was with Hunter. I'd always been more worried about Ramsey's love for the cameras than whether he was fucking around.

"Dottie was looking for you." Hunter didn't sound any more forgiving than I was inclined to be.

"I found her. Thanks. I really am sorry." Ramsey's expression softened.

Hunter nodded. "I knew what I was signing up for."

Somehow, I'd managed to forget. Or at least diminish the memories until they felt insignificant.

Ramsey turned to me. "It's a universal apology. To both of you. How are things going?"

"I met the CEO of Insignia Oil. He stared at my tits the entire time he told me what great taste you had in causes. But at least I wasn't the only one objectified. The woman brought in to fix the Digital Media problems loves Hunter's ass in those trousers."

"I'd have a hard time arguing with either of them." Ramsey's light tone said he wanted to laugh this off and move on. "I really am sorry, Violet. I've been trying to nail this interview down for months, and it just happened to fall tonight."

Hunter's snort was soft. "Go, Debbie."

Ramsey twisted his mouth. Watching them not-argue was almost worse than arguing with Ramsey myself. "And?" Ramsey asked.

"I'm interviewing more people the day after tomorrow," Hunter said and looked at me. "I can fire her if I find someone at least as good to take her place."

That seemed fair. "You dropped almost everything, to make this happen. I can't fault you that one or two things couldn't be pushed, especially if you didn't know about them."

"So we're all good." Ramsey stood.

It seemed that way. I didn't feel any lingering animosity.

"Do you want to get out of here?" he asked.

The idea of leaving definitely made it better. "Can we do that?"

"Things are winding down. The doors close in less than two hours. Dottie has her own *Hunter*, who set all of this up with the staff, and will make sure it all comes down." Ramsey made it sound so easy.

Hunter pushed away from the table and tugged me to my feet. "It's a fair point. I vote for leaving."

"I really feel like I should stay." This was my party. I should be here until the end.

running for it

"What are you going to do if you do stay?" Ramsey asked.

"Be here?"

He grabbed my other hand. "Not a good answer. Give me something more concrete than, *I have to help*."

"Isn't that enough?" I didn't have anything else.

"Nope. They've got this covered." Ramsey led us farther from the crowd, toward a rear exit.

We took the elevator up to the same floor as earlier. And stopped in front of the same room. I'd never even thought to ask if we were all staying together, though I hoped so. Would that be an issue if someone dug into Ramsey? People did that in politics, right? Had he reserved three separate rooms, to only use one?

"You two looked good together tonight." Ramsey's comment interrupted my rambling thoughts. "Like you were having fun."

"We were," I said.

"Someone had to keep the guest of honor company, while you were occupied," Hunter said. "Besides, Violet's way better to talk to than most of those assholes."

"Fair point." Ramsey opened the door and let us step past him. "I feel like I should make it up to you." He spun on me the moment we were all inside, pressing me to the wall with his body and trapping me in place.

I knew this look. This posture. The heat and playfulness in Ramsey's gaze. The possessiveness. My pulse raced in the most delicious way, but I was going to poke the bear a little more. Especially after he'd vanished for so long. "No need. Hunter kept me satisfied."

"Really?" Ramsey slid two fingers into my mouth, and I sucked instinctively. "So you don't need me?"

I shrugged, unable to say much with my mouth full.

The sound of fabric tearing filled the room when Ramsey ripped the slit of my dress with his free hand. He dropped his wet fingers to tease my bare pussy. "So I should just let the two of you go at it?" he asked, as he slipped between my folds.

His closeness and touch, and the threat in his voice made me slick with need.

"I should sit back and watch, while he slides his fat cock in your tight, wet pussy." Ramsey dipped his fingers inside me, and I thrust into the penetration.

I couldn't find my voice, as he pumped in me. When he pulled out, I felt empty, and I wanted more. This time he shoved his fingers, slick with my juices, in Hunter's mouth. Watching Hunter suck him clean made me squeeze my thighs together.

running for it

"I think I like that idea." Ramsey's voice was low and suggestive. "Letting Hunter spill his load in you. Licking you clean after. Tasting both of you, while you writhe against my tongue.

I was pretty sure that was a submissive kind of thing, but there was nothing submissive in Ramsey's posture or words.

"Would you like that, Taffy? Me, between your legs, sucking Hunter's cum from your pussy?"

I licked my lips and nodded.

Ramsey turned to Hunter.

"I do like fucking Violet almost as much as I like seeing you on your knees," Hunter said.

How was this the hottest thing I'd ever been involved in, when we'd barely crested *foreplay*?

Chapter Thirteen

Hunter traced his thumb along my jaw, holding my gaze, and our conversation from earlier rushed back.

He dipped his head, lips millimeters from mine. "I meant all the good things. I want you here," he murmured so softly I barely heard him, before claiming my mouth in a soft kiss. Hunter wasn't rough like Ramsey, but his intensity and deliberate movements were their own kinds of arousing. He lay barely-there kisses along my bare shoulders and chest. Up my neck as he removed the necklace and set it aside. He let his nails glide lightly down my spine as he unzipped my dress and let it fall to the floor.

Goosebumps covered every inch of my completely exposed body. I was on display in nothing but my lace-up heels, and *fuck* it made me wet.

Hunter moved to my front, to kiss down my chest, over my hips, along the tops of my thighs. The slow burn was excruciatingly delicious. He unlaced

running for it

my shoes one at a time, barely touching my calves, and had me step out of the heels so he could set them aside.

The only contact he made was with not-particularly erogenous bits, but I was slick with need, and my chest heaved with each breath of anticipation.

Hunter stood and brushed his lips over mine. He gripped my wrists and raised my hands to kiss my palms. "Can I trust you not to touch anything? Not even yourself?"

"You're asking a lot, but I'll do it for you," I teased. My desire was amplified by Ramsey's silence. I couldn't see him, but he was here watching everything.

Hunter let go of me and put some distance between us. He was as methodical about undressing himself as he had been me. Tie off first and set aside. Cuff links safely on the dresser. Belt whipped out with just enough snap to send a pleasant shiver down my spine. Shirt untucked and unbuttoned.

This was the most low-key, seductive striptease I'd ever seen, and Hunter did it all while watching my flushed and naked body. When he stripped off the remainder of this clothes, he was already hard, his cock thick and long and standing at attention.

He moved in for another kiss, as soft and simple as before, but he pressed closely this time, his bare skin searing against mine.

I reached to stroke his erection as it dug into my stomach, and he clucked.

"You promised no touching." The calm warning in his voice was like fingertips dancing over my skin. He caught my wrists, grabbed his tie, and bound my arms in front of me.

Sexy, but ineffective. "I can still do plenty like this."

Hunter gripped the knot and lead me by the writs to a nearby chair. As he sat he draped my arms over his shoulders, then grabbed my hips, guiding me to straddle his legs.

I felt like I was barely balanced, but he held me steady, guiding his dick between us rather than inside me. He didn't stop me from grinding into him. Letting his cock slip along my wet pussy and tease my clit. The build left me lightheaded. Desperate. If this were Ramsey I'd beg. It may not get me what I asked for, but it would up the ante.

Something told me Hunter had a specific plan, and it would be worth riding out.

He half-prompted half-lifted me enough to penetrate me, gliding in easily and stretching me out. When he was buried inside, he hit that perfect spot that tingled from my toes all the way to my

running for it

fingertips. He reached between us to tease my clit while I rocked against him.

I was already near bursting from the build-up, the pressure of his touch, his cock in me, the way he raked his gaze over me, drew me to a fast, hard orgasm. I clenched around him, wanting more.

As he eased away from my clit, he increased the pace, slamming inside me, drawing out my climax until the world was a blur and my head was lost in clouds of pleasure.

Hunter crushed his mouth to mine, nipping my lips and sucking on my tongue. His restraint was gone. He dragged his mouth down my chest, to scrape his teeth over my nipples until it stung, then moved back to my lips. "I won't last long," he murmured between grunts. "You feel too good."

With all this build-up, I'd lost all sense of time anyway. And I was going to beg after all. "Come inside me. Please."

"Fuck. Fuck, yes." Hunter grunted and gripped my hips hard. He pounded me. Harder. Faster. He was close. And then his stuttered gasp told me he'd come too, spilling inside me.

The frantic need tapered, slowing and then stopping as we did. Hunter rested his forehead against my chest, his heavy breathing matching mine.

That was incredible. *Wow*. Anticipation still hummed through me, though. More waited for me. Could I handle more?

And then Ramsey was there, naked and knotting his fingers in Hunter's short hair. Yanking his head back and kissing him hard.

Hunter twitched inside me, even as he was softening.

Yeah, I could take a bit more.

Ramsey unbound my wrists and gently took my hands. "Can you stand?"

I wasn't sure I could talk yet, and I might be wobbly on my legs, but I could manage. I nodded, and let him help me to my feet.

He fisted my hair, yanking my head back and drawing a whimper from me. He kissed me hard, before sucking down my neck to bite the soft skin where it met my shoulder. "Every time you look in the mirror"—he growled—"every time you brush your fingers over that tender skin, remember who put this here."

"What about when it fades?" Thankfully my voice came back in time for me to sass.

"I'll have to replace it before then." Ramsey lifted me into his arms, carried me the short distance to the bed, and set me in the middle, moving pillows to prop up my head.

running for it

Ramsey knelt between my legs and forced them apart. His rough kisses up the inside of my thighs said the teasing was done. This was hungry and desperate, and when he dove his tongue into my pussy, my hips bucked and I thrust into his face.

It wasn't only that his touch was enticing—that would leave me panting anyway—but knowing he was tasting Hunter on me. That he was licking me clean like I was the most delicious delicacy.

Ramsey took his time, sucking, devouring, until I was writhing against his face and whimpering. When he glided higher, to wrap his lips around my clit, a fresh shock jolted through me. I screamed when I came, gripping the short strands of his hair tight, and holding him in place until his touch was too much.

Ramsey moved up my body to claim my mouth in a messy, slippery, tantalizing kiss. Goddess, we tasted good.

He pulled back and his fevered gaze met mine, stealing breath I didn't think I had left. He pinned my knees to my chest and pushed inside me. It was a fast, frantic fuck. Skin slapping against skin, moans mingling in the air, and gasps of desire.

I shouldn't have another orgasm in me, but there it was, yanking me into the most delicious oblivion of stars and galaxies dancing in front of my eyes.

Ramsey spilled inside me, gripping the backs of my thighs hard enough to bruise. It was all part of the bliss, and I didn't want to come back down.

When the frantic pace slowed again, then stopped, the haze remained, wrapping up my thoughts while Ramsey covered me with playful kisses. He vanished for a few seconds, and returned to clean me up, tenderly wiping away a mixture of juices.

He fell into the bed next to me, and Hunter joined us. It was one big, warm pile of adoration, I felt theirs for each other as strongly as I felt my own.

I was so glad I'd decided to do this—to give Ramsey and me another chance. I'd missed this feeling. This closeness. Obviously the sex, but everything else too. Ramsey's presence. His company. Pretty much everything about him.

Except for that one thing that drove us apart last time. That thing I refused to name tonight, because in this room I could pretend it didn't exist. As long as tonight lasted, everything was perfect.

Chapter Fourteen

I wasn't a pass-out-immediately-after-sex kind of person, but it usually numbed my brain. Tonight, though, as I lay curled up with Ramsey and Hunter, I didn't want to fall asleep. This moment was perfect, and in the morning, it wouldn't be.

"Do you turn into a pumpkin in the morning?" Ramsey asked.

It was a silly, poorly-phrased question, but I knew him well enough to recognize the meaning mirrored my thoughts. "Lyn made me take the day off, so I don't have anywhere to be tomorrow.

"We should go be tourists." Hunter didn't sound tired either.

Just the thought of walking made my feet ache. "Not in those heels."

"You have other shoes," Ramsey said. "In fact, I'd bet you packed clothes, even though I told you not to."

"I'm not taking that bet. It would be a poor way to start off a night on the strip, gambling on a loser."

Hunter raised a hand, worked his jaw, then dropped his hand. "I'm not sure that makes as much sense as you think."

"But you got my meaning."

Ramsey sat up, tugging both of us with him. "Let's go. Get dressed." He was already on his feet. He grabbed his trousers and a tiny box fell out.

"What's that?" Hunter's suspicion amplified my ambivalence.

"It's from Dottie." Ramsey opened the velvet wrapped box to reveal a stunning ring nestled inside. The cluster of diamonds was as big as my thumb. "It's been in the family forever. She wants me to give it to the person I marry." *Person.* His wording may have been gender neutral, but the ring wasn't.

Even if it were, it was only going to fit one finger at a time. "It's pretty." I tried to keep my tone light.

"Uh-huh. Stunning," Hunter said flatly as he pulled on his jeans.

Ramsey snapped the box shut again. "What was I going to tell her?"

I didn't have that answer, but I suspected if we kept this up for any amount of time, we'd need to figure it out.

Hunter took the ring from Ramsey, and shoved it in his pocket. "I'll make sure it gets put in a safe."

running for it

We finished dressing, and headed down to the strip. When we stepped outside, the magic that had started to evaporate, the pocket of the world I wanted to stay in as long as I could, was bright and vibrant again. I loved the lights of Vegas at night. I loved that even at one in the morning, there were people everywhere.

And as Ramsey wrapped arms around both our waists, I loved that no one knew us. There were no expectations for how any of us had to act.

"Where to first?" I was happy to just look. Wander. Escape with them. I was even willing to ignore my aching feet to have a few more hours of this.

"You know what I've always wanted?" Hunter leaned into Ramsey, nudging him into me and pushing all of us in a new direction. "Okay, not always, but let's call it that."

I had a few guesses, but no concrete idea. "Chocolate covered strippers?"

He laughed. "Definitely not. This relationship has the perfect number of dicks in it. I want my boyfriend to win me a prize at Circus Circus."

"Ooh, me too." It was childish and ridiculous and I loved the idea.

Ramsey snorted. "Not sure what makes you think I'm capable of that. Hunter's the athlete." He led us through the front doors of Circus Circus anyway.

"Ramsey Miller can do anything he sets his mind to." Right now, I had no doubt.

"Ooh, I like that as a campaign slogan. We should have Debbie put that on all your pages," Hunter said.

We followed the signs that said *Arcade* past slot machines, tables, and restaurants.

Ramsey shook his head. "Fuck Debbie."

"Do. Not." Hunter's voice went hard.

A giggle slipped past my lips without my permission, and I bit it off. We were still joking, weren't we?

Ramsey and Hunter both laughed, and I joined back in. This was like being drunk. Great, now I wanted to drink. No reason I couldn't. No one was relying on me to be sober tonight. We'd already done the *absolutely scorching* sex thing.

We pulled up short in front of the arcade, and the laughter stopped. No lights were on, and the security gates were down.

Hunter pouted. That was adorable.

"Apparently I can't do everything." Ramsey was almost surprised. "Oh, I have a better idea." He looked at Hunter. "You know that thing you said you wanted to see?"

running for it

Hunter shrugged. "The life sized Gundam in Japan?"

My laughter was back.

"With Violet," Ramsey said, pointing us back toward the main floor.

Wait. What?

Hunter shook his head. "She'd never."

"I'd never what?"

"She might if we put a few drinks in her first." Ramsey kept talking as if I hadn't said a word.

Which I didn't appreciate. "Given what the two of you just did to me—with me, in me, on me—I don't think I need to be drunk for much."

Hunter sucked in a sharp breath. "You say that."

"You're killing me. You know that, right? I'm dead with curiosity..." I trailed off when we stopped at the edge of a pit, next to a Texas Hold 'em table.

"We'll start small, have a couple drinks, and work our way up." Ramsey finally looked at me. "Hunter thinks you could compete. I tend to think he's right."

I thought that too, when I was winning one hand after another against friends. But Hunter was right about something else. "I'd definitely need to be drunk to believe that. This isn't just for laughs around the kitchen table."

"Nope. It's better." Ramsey pointed me toward a chair. "Five hundred in chips," he said to the dealer.

What? "I can—"

Ramsey crushed his mouth to mine, cutting me off and stilling my thoughts.

I sighed when he pulled away.

"You can." He nudged me until I sat.

I bid the minimum allowed with the first hand. Just me against the dealer. When I won, I left the money on the table for the next round, and Ramsey handed me a whiskey sour to celebrate.

The wins kept adding up until they didn't. I frowned when I lost hand number nine.

Ramsey rested his hand on the back of my chair. "You've still got chips. Might as well play until they're gone or you're tired of the game."

"But the two of you—

"Are fascinated," Hunter said. "Keep playing."

So I did. I lost track of how many hands I won or lost. Sometimes the chip pile was almost nothing, and others it was intoxicatedly large.

The drinks kept coming, too. Until I was making more mistakes than I should be. Until I was giggling more than I should be. Until more people were joining the table, because we'd flown past late night and into early morning.

My head was light and I was giggling maybe more than I should be, but the guy who had joined about five hands ago? Totally bluffing, and I was going to win big.

running for it

I put all my chips on the line. Not that I had a bunch left, but if I won, I'd be close to the five-hundred dollar mark I started at.

He flipped his cards, and I frowned.

Nope. He hadn't been bluffing.

"C'mon, Taffy." Ramsey tugged my sleeve.

I sighed in resignation, but it had been fun. When I stepped from my stool, my head swam. Oh, pretty lights. I stumbled and Hunter caught me with a laugh.

"We need coffee." He leaned as much weight on me as I did him as the three of us made our way to the main floor.

Ramsey tapped Hunter lightly on the nose. "See why I love those smarts? That's why he runs things. Always on top of the details."

"Love. That's sweet. You two are an adorable couple." I swayed my hips, and something hard bit into me when I bumped into Hunter. "Is that a… something benign in your pocket, or are you just happy to see me?"

"Only you, Taffy, would use a word like benign while you're completely drunk," Ramsey teased.

"I'm not drunk. You're drunk." I was a little drunk.

Hunter nudged me upright to reach into his pocket. "Oh." His tone went flat. He was holding the ring from Dottie. "I wasn't supposed to bring this with me."

"You know what sucks most about that thing?" Ramsey was suddenly sad. "I'm expected to use that. I can't hand it to Ravyn, who'll look amazing in it no matter who she marries. I'm supposed to fall in love with some woman who doesn't mind the trophy life wife—" his laugh was sad "—wife life, and who we like each other enough to exchange rings." He watched Hunter the entire time he spoke.

I felt bad for him. For them. "When you put it that way, it would be easier for Hunter and I to get married." I meant the comment to be funny. To lighten the mood. I was met with two blank stares. "I know. I'm not saying that. I'm just saying, no one's watching us like they watch Ramsey."

"Must be nice." Ramsey sighed.

***

Sunlight struck my face, and I pulled the covers over my head to block it out. My head throbbed in protest at the sudden movement.

"Did we… step in front of a train last night? This morning?" Hunter's question was as sluggish as my thoughts.

Ramsey groaned. "What is that beeping?"

"Your phone. Pretty sure," Hunter said.

running for it

My gut lurched up, then down, then in a circle over and over. I was less than delicate untangling myself from the men as I raced into the bathroom. As I was emptying the contents of my stomach, my hair was pulled back. Ramsey gently rubbed my back.

When I was spent, I sank back onto the floor, and prayed for the room to stop spinning. Thankfully no one had turned on the lights.

Hunter handed me a glass of water, and returned to leaning against the wall and rubbing his forehead.

Ramsey sat next on my left, mimicking my knees-to-the-chest posture.

"Neither of you look violently ill." I was a little jealous of that.

Hunter rolled his neck. "We drink casually more often than you. But God, it's been a long time since I got black-out drunk."

Ramsey slipped his right hand under my left. "Oh, shit." He held both up.

I looked down to see Dottie's ring on my finger, and my stomach curdled again. "I'm just holding this, right?" Snippets of early this morning trickled back.

"Maybe the two of you should get married. Imagine how much that eases concerns about sneaking around." Ramsey sounded sad.

Hunter's face was illuminated by his phone as he scrolled through. His string of *shit, shit, shit* got louder the longer he stared. "I don't think you're just holding it."

"I'm not agreeing to this," I argued.

Hunter tilted my chin and met my gaze. "Please? Marry me?"

When we'd gotten to the chapel, they wanted a marriage license, and the courthouse wasn't open yet. Did that stop us?

"Hang on. I know a guy." Ramsey already had his phone out.

I swallowed hard as my gut threatened to revolt again. Holy fuck. I'd married my ex-but-not-boyfriend's boyfriend.

Chapter Fifteen

This would be fine. Between Hunter and I, we could plan anything, and Ramsey was a master of executing those ideas—even when we were too drunk to think right apparently. This didn't even require a complex plan. "We can get it annulled? Do we even have to do that much? We can just ask the chapel not to file the paperwork? No one but us knows about this."

"About that…" Hunter was still staring at his phone. "These photos? They're on the *Miller for Senate* social media pages.

"How—" Ramsey was on his feet in a flash, bolting back into the bedroom. "*Shit*." His shout echoed through the entire suite.

I pulled myself up to sit on the edge of the tub. Given the situation, this seemed like a good place to talk about it.

Ramsey returned and handed me my phone. "So, you know that interview I did last night?" He was uncharacteristically sheepish.

"Yes…" I was torn between checking my phone now and flushing it before I saw if I was caught in the fallout. I wouldn't be able to think until I knew, though.

"I saved some photos from the interview to a shared cloud folder. And I saved the wedding photos to the same place, so Debbie shared them."

As Ramsey spoke, I saw the text from Luna. It just said *congratulations.* There was no *!!!* No :) In Luna speak, it said *fuck you.* "No," the word tumbled past my lips. She thought I'd hidden this from her.

"I don't care where you accidentally put them. Debbie had no right." Hunter's anger grabbed my attention again. He jabbed his screen hard enough I wondered if he was cracking the glass, the brought the phone to his ear. There was a short pause. "Save it." He clipped off the word. "No part of my personal life crosses into Ramsey's campaign… I don't give a fuck what you found there… Bullshit. You knew better… No. Don't do *anything* until you hear from one of us." He disconnected and swung his arm as if he wanted to throw the phone. Then pressed it to his hip, as if looking for a pocket.

Right. We were all still naked. I pushed to my feet, legs shaking from uncertainty rather than hangover. "I'm going to get dressed." I walked past both of them. The numbness in my mind was going

running for it

to vanish any minute now. The panic would set in. I'd rather be wearing clothes when it did.

I yanked on panties. A bra and T-shirt. Jeans.

Numbness was still there. I sank onto the edge of the bed.

Ramsey and Hunter were shirtless, but at least they'd tucked away the dangly bits. How distracted was I that I didn't care if their dicks were hanging out?

"We have to undo this." I was stating the obvious, but I couldn't find anything smarter.

"It's not going to be that easy," Ramsey said.

I started at him as if he were speaking a foreign language. He must be, because the words coming out of his mouth didn't make any sense. "It's very much that easy if Hunter and I both agree. I had a friend go through a no-fault divorce. We sign some paperwork—a lot of paperwork—and we're done."

"Or, we could stick to the plan we made last night." Ramsey was still speaking in gibberish. "The one where this makes things easier."

I blinked several times, until he was a blur, then squeezed my eyes shut and watched the sparkles behind my eyelids. I finally looked at him again. "This is what I'm hearing—*we got drunk and did something stupid. Let's all lie to everyone and tell them we meant it.* Do you remember why you and I broke up?"

"Vividly."

"And you're asking me to lie to the entire world—not just a few cameras—and tell them this entire thing was on purpose. You want me to stay with Hunter because… Why? Not that I dislike you, Hunter, but marriage?"

Hunter puffed out his cheeks and sucked them in when he sighed. "I get it. No explanation necessary."

"That makes one of us, because I need to know why you're not taking my side."

"There are rumors about Hunter and I," Ramsey said. "People are noticing what we are. The rumors are quiet now, but they're getting louder."

I was clearly missing something. "So own it. "Maybe it's time—"

"This marriage isn't a big deal." Ramsey sounded like he believed that. "I'm only asking that you play along until we—"

"Figure out how to spin a divorce?" I didn't appreciate being talked over. "If it wasn't a big deal, you wouldn't be asking me to play along."

Ramsey frowned. "Please, Violet."

I couldn't… What was going on? "If you ask me to do this, to pretend I'm married to someone I wouldn't otherwise choose, for your political career, and I do it? That's the end of us." I hated the words, but I meant them. I wouldn't out Ramsey and Hunter,

running for it

but what they were asking me to do was a personal line I wouldn't cross just so he could be elected.

"He's not doing it for his campaign." Hunter's voice was quiet. "He's doing it for me."

Was it possible to drink oneself into an alternate dimension?

"Are you sure?" Ramsey asked.

Hunter nodded.

"Fill me in. *Now*." Before this drove me over the edge.

Hunter pressed his back to the closest wall and turned his gaze to the ceiling. "It took me a long time to figure out my preferences, and I'll be honest, I didn't put a lot of thought into it when I was younger. My parents are religious, and so was the community I was raised in. If you think *hetero* is the default assumption, multiply that by one-hundred and press that weight on a kid whose entire world expected *great things* from him."

I'd seen that before. I'd heard it from more than one of the kids in my shelter. There was what most people experienced just from existing, and then there was being paired with the opposite sex from the time a kid was old enough to walk, for appearances. For *isn't that cute? Isn't he such a lady killer?* Moments.

"Anyway." Hunter sighed again. "Fast forward through a couple of decades of denial that I've told my therapist about so you don't need to hear it, and a series of events that forced the pieces to fit, and I realized I'd been in love with my best friend for as long as I could remember. Telling Ramsey was the most frightening thing I'd ever done."

I couldn't be jealous of that. Not of the pain or sincerity in Hunter's story.

"Fortunately that went well," Ramsey said and squeezed Hunter's hand.

Hunter's mouth twitched in an unformed smile. "He went with me to tell Mom, and that was the second scariest, because she'd always been my biggest supporter." His frown was back. "She dropped a bombshell on me, too. Assured me first she still loved me. All the stuff a parent is supposed to say, but Dad had been diagnosed with Pancreatic cancer less than a week earlier. *This will ruin your father*, she said. *You know how he is*."

"I'm sorry." My sympathy felt ineffective, but I didn't have anything else to offer.

Hunter tugged his hand free from Ramsey and crossed his arms. "He only had six months to live. Mom begged me not to send my father to his grave knowing his only boy was queer."

Goddess, my heart was breaking for Hunter.

"Dad's still with us, thank God." Hunter's smile didn't reach his eyes. "But he hasn't recovered, he's simply holding on because he's a tough bastard. And

running for it

every chance my mother gets, she reminds me, *begs me*, to keep the secret just a little longer."

I couldn't believe I was considering going along with this, but the reasons had changed, and I'd heard variations of Hunter's story—seen the negative fallout—too many times to fault him for his decision. "How long are we talking?"

"After the elections, Hunter will be out of the public eye. No scrutiny. No one is going to notice or care if he quietly divorces, and his parents will think he gave marriage a try." *After the elections*. Ramsey wasn't talking about the primaries.

"November?" I couldn't hide my disbelief. "It's *January*."

"November is the worst case scenario, right Ramsey?" Hunter's voice was pointed. He didn't want to be married to me any more than I did him. "We're not going to stop looking for solutions. All I'm asking is that you work with me on a plan that doesn't involve having papers drawn up *right now*."

Money and connections get things done, but frequently not the important things. Hunter's words from the plane bounced into my thoughts. Something neither he nor Ramsey ever did, remind me of the favors they'd done for me in the past. I was going to do this. Please don't let me regret it. "Okay. But the ring?" I held up my hand. "I can't wear this." It was Ramsey's ring for fuck's sake, and now that it was on my finger, I could admit to myself I'd hoped it would end up there. But not like this.

"Of course not," Hunter said quickly. "We'll get you something more appropriate to us."

"You can't tell *anyone* this isn't real." Leave it to Ramsey to drive home how important the facade was.

More pieces of reality sank in. "But our friends…" Shared friends, thanks to Lyn's relationship with Owen and Kingston. "When Hunter and I *break up*…"

"We'll tell them this is why there's been friction between you and me, because of you and Hunter." Ramsey had figured too much of this out too quickly. "But on this trip we talked, and we're all friends again. And then you'll have an amicable break-up."

Which would make it harder to be with Ramsey after. This was such a fucking mess. "I have to tell Luna. I won't lie to her."

"I'm fine with it as long as she will be," Hunter said.

I still didn't know if I was.

Chapter Sixteen

Talking to Luna, making things right with her, was my top priority. I sent her a text, *We'll talk as soon as I get home. This afternoon. I'm sorry.*

Her reply was instant—*it's fine.*

All lower case. Period at the end. She was furious with me.

Hunter had a slew of messages to sift through, and a lot of them were from family who wanted to know more about this mystery *Violet* woman. The one from his mother said *Not Ramsey's ex-Violet.*

My other texts and voicemails were more happy sounding than Luna's. Various versions of *Congratulations.* Lyn's made my stomach churn all over again. *You should have asked for more time off. It's not a big deal. Take a honeymoon. Enjoy each other.*

No, no, no. I already hated walking away from work with short notice yesterday and today.

We don't want to make a big deal out of things. It's why we kept things secret. As I typed, I shared the message with Hunter and Ramsey. Hunter was doing the same so we knew that we weren't giving anyone conflicting information. This was one reason lying sucked so much.

Lyn replied. *It's okay. Take the days. At least the rest of the week.*

I couldn't. That would devour me. *Please don't make me do that. I'll be there tomorrow, like I'm supposed to.*

Lyn's *Fine. I can't force you to not come in* wasn't as fatal sounding as Luna's, but it still made me frown.

Ramsey didn't have many messages, especially considering the news went out on his accounts. One was from Kingston, asking if Ramsey was okay with Hunter and me, and one was a voicemail from Ravyn. Ramsey played the short snippet for us.

"Really?" Ravyn's tone was flat.

She wasn't buying it. Smart woman.

As we packed, rode to the airport, and got on the plane, the conversation was all *next steps.* Tension tightened in my neck and throbbed in my skull with each new thing I had to do or remember. Any peace I'd achieved over the last day was gone, and I just wanted to curl up in a leather plane seat and sleep for a billion years.

We'd tell people a story that was mostly-true, but still had to open with a lie. Hunter and I had been together for a while, and that was why Ramsey and I

running for it

clashed. Partly because of my past with Ramsey but largely because he'd hated keeping my relationship with Hunter a secret.

When my barking laugh slipped out at the last bit, Ramsey shot me a withering glare. I shrugged. "At least own it with those of us who know better."

"So, Violet should keep her apartment." Hunter interrupted before Ramsey could counter. "But she'll need to move in with me. We can take our time, but anything you need, I'll have brought in," he looked at me.

"And when people ask *why now?*" I couldn't imagine anyone would buy this story.

"Vegas, especially the party, made the two of you see how tired you were of hiding the truth and keeping your distance, so you let impulse take over." Ramsey's immediate answer wasn't a surprise, but at least his flat tone said he didn't like this arrangement either. "You meant to tell your families and friends first, but someone leaked the news.

Ramsey raked his fingers through his hair. "Fame is fleeting if you're not pursuing it. If your relationship isn't constantly on display, people will forget."

"Our friends and family won't forget. And not many will understand if it looks like I went from you to Hunter and back to you."

The longer we lived this lie, the harder the break-up would be on everyone around us. The harder it would be to find my way back to Ramsey without questions. Yeah, I went years without seeing him, but twenty-four hours ago I was excited to be giving us another try.

"This gets shittier the longer I think about it." Hunter couldn't have echoed my thoughts more perfectly.

"We'll find a solution fast," Ramsey said. "We'll keep our explanations brief. Stay low-key."

I didn't believe it. "You're not capable of low-key."

"I am for the two of you." Ramsey's sincerity would have meant more if this entire conversation were about anything else.

We landed in Salt Lake far too soon for my liking.

Hunter would take me to Luna's, and then back to my place to pack enough to stay at his.

When we reached the house where Luna rented the basement, I asked Hunter to drop me off. "I need to have this conversation alone."

"I get that. I'll be at the coffee shop a few blocks down. Call me when you're ready to go."

I nodded. Before I could climb from the car, he grabbed my hand and tugged me back.

running for it

He pressed his lips to my forehead. "I know this is a universally bad idea, but there's no one I'd rather be accidentally married to. We'll figure this out fast."

"Okay." I couldn't think of anything better to say.

I heard his car drive away as I headed up the side path and down the stairs to Luna's door. I knocked, and waited.

There was no answer, but Luna's car was in the driveway. The curtains in the tiny window next to the door moved. Probably not the wind.

I knocked again. Still nothing.

I sent Luna a text. *Please talk to me.*

I'm not home, she replied.

The exchange would have made me smile if I weren't so stressed. *I didn't say I was at your apartment. Please let me in. I'll explain.*

You don't have to explain to me who you love.

As I read Luna's reply, I heard the deadbolt *thunk*. The door opened, but there was no Luna. I stepped inside.

"Congratulations." Luna's flat tone startled me. She swung the door shut behind me. "I would have gotten you a wedding present if you'd ever even bothered to mention you were dating him, let alone in love enough to get married. But I'm sure your boyfriend—husband—will shower you with all sorts of gifts."

"It's not real." Goddess it felt good to say that. I turned to find Luna standing with her back to the door and her arms crossed.

Her frown deepened. "What's not?"

"You have to promise not to tell anyone, and please don't be mad at me. Please." The day's stress weighed me down and made my voice crack.

Luna's expression softened. "I promise I won't tell anyone, and I won't be mad." Her tone was kind. "What's not real?"

I collapsed on the couch. "This all stays between us."

"Always."

I didn't know how far back to go. Too much had happened since that first charity dinner, leaving a smear in my memory. "So... Ramsey and Hunter are a couple, and they don't want anyone to know, because Hunter's dad doesn't know he's gay—bi? Pan?—and Ramsey and I were going to try dating too, not exclusive, cuz of the whole Hunter thing, and all three of us were good with it. And then last night we had way too many free drinks and decided it would be a lot easier to keep all of our secrets if Hunter and I got married and the news got leaked and now we have to figure out how to do damage control and end this thing without too many people getting hurt and Goddess, I am *never* drinking again."

running for it

Luna studied me with sympathy. "It's my fault, isn't it?"

"What? *No.* How would this be your fault?"

"Ramsey told you what he did for me, and he forced you to do this in return?"

Apparently my day could get more fucked-up. "What did Ramsey do for you?"

"Oh."

Not the answer I wanted. "Luna?"

She perched on the arm of the couch, feet on the cushion next to me, and stared at her fingers. "I don't know for certain it was him, but I don't know who else it could have been, so I always assumed he did it to win you back."

"*Luna?*" Had I missed the Alice-in-Wonderland-style *Drink Me* label on those drinks last night?

"Remember when I was arrested, and my plea bargain and sentence were so much more lenient than we expected?"

Pieces were clicking for me. "Yeah..."

"My public defender and the ADA implied they'd heard from a friend that I wasn't a risk. They recommended the judge go light on me. That happened two days after you broke up with Ramsey and was exactly the opposite of what I'd been threatened with up to that point."

"You never told me."

Luna finally met my gaze. "I figured you knew. Why would Ramsey do that unless he was using it to win you back?"

I didn't know. Unless he really did it just to help Luna.

"If you want me to keep this quiet, I will," Luna said. "You don't have to explain yourself, I know you have a good reason for it. But I'll help you find a way out. Also"—she ducked her head—"I'm sorry in advance." Her last words were quiet.

I couldn't handle any more surprises today. "What did you do?"

"I called Lyn."

"And?"

"I told her we should throw you a huge surprise party, to celebrate your wedding, and surprise you as a thanks for *your* surprise."

It was no mistake she'd said *surprise* three times. I hated surprise parties.

Luna shrugged. "I was *really* mad." She must have been.

"It's okay. I promise to act surprised. It's no big deal." But it was one more thing to deal with. I sighed. "I don't know what to do. I made these promises, I had a good reason, but… this sucks."

"You could get stuck with a worse guy than Hunter." Luna offered a weak smile.

running for it

It was true. "But I don't want to be *stuck* with anyone."

"Do you want to ask the cards?" Luna was already looking at the shelf where she kept her favorite tarot decks on display.

I didn't believe in the mysticism, though there was no reason to stop Luna from doing so. I was willing to admit that more than one of her readings had opened my mind to new possibilities and given me direction I wouldn't have seen otherwise. "Sure. Can we do one of the pretty decks?"

Luna grabbed a manga tarot, and led me to the kitchen table. She handed me the cards. "You know how it works. Focus on your question, shuffle, three times, and then cut the deck and hand it back."

My question may be too vague, but it was the best I had. *How do I get out of this*?

I handed Luna back the deck. "Hunter and Ramsey are together."

"Not anymore apparently." Luna's retort was dry but amused. She looked at me with a frown. "Sorry. Inappropriate."

"Everything about this is. They're not out—obviously—and they're keeping it a secret because of Hunter's family, so I agreed to help them keep the secret, because all I could think about…"

Luna frowned. "Was Eva, I know. And you really don't have to explain."

"I owe you at least that much."

Luna gave me a soft smile, then laid out the cards—one, then three, then one.

I frowned at how many were upside down. That didn't seem like a good thing. And one was The Fool. That had to be bad. "You usually only give me 3 cards."

"This is for clarity. I have a feeling you need some of that."

I really did. "Okay, tell me it's not as bad as it looks."

"It's never as bad as you think it is," Luna said. "And neither is this. The situation or the cards." She pointed to the first one. I knew enough about the images and numbers to know it was the Three of Wands. "The question we're asking this card is, what aren't you seeing clearly? Yes, you've made some choices, you've set things in motion, but that doesn't mean your story is done. You still have time to decide—which you excel at—and write the ending. You still have time to make it good, instead of bad."

"That sounds hopeful." One thing I could always count on Luna for was seeing the silver lining. "But what about him?" I pointed to the upside-down Fool."

"That's you."

I scowled. "Thanks."

running for it

Luna gave a light laugh. "It's still not bad. You're the hero of this story, and your intuition will guide you. But you've got a lot of doubt, which is fair. You've let fear take the reins in the past, but you can still follow your heart toward an answer."

That was almost sappy. And left me with a strange blend of hope and confusion. "Give me more." The next card was the Seven of Cups, inverted.

"Yes, ma'am. You're looking for a solution to let you be at peace with the current situation—"

"I'm really not. I want it over with."

Luna looked at me with her eyebrows raised. "Over is still a solution, one of many. And you have *so many* choices here. But you can't have your cake and eat it too. Some are fantasy, some are realistic, and some will destroy you. Don't let your fears and daydreams get in the way of what you're truly capable of."

I didn't have *that* many choices. Stay with Hunter and live the lie, or divorce him and let him deal with the fallout, since the entire world knew apparently already knew about our mistake.

"You're questioning me." Luna didn't sound upset.

"I'm not. The cards, maybe."

She smiled. "You don't *have* to listen, but try not to write it all off too quickly." She pointed to the next one, an Eight of Coins, also upside down. "You can still influence the situation. You haven't lost control."

That was the most comforting thing I'd heard today. "Okay…?"

"This is your chance to master something you're already good at, but it's going to take work, and it's going to hurt. Don't settle. Don't let yourself get dragged into the unfulfilling. Push past the pain points, and you'll be happier and stronger for it."

That just sounded like smart life advice. Or painful life advice. Then again, I was a bit of a masochist.

"What's the last one?" I asked. Besides an inverted Knight of Swords.

Luna sighed and tapped the card lightly with one fingernail. "Probably Ramsey."

That wasn't fair. "I have to be a fool and he gets to be a knight?"

"I already told you The Fool isn't bad. This though… has the potential to be destructive." Her voice got quiet toward the end.

I hated the sound of that. "You said there were no bad answers."

"I said it isn't as bad as it looks. Things can still go wrong if you let them. But this is all about possibility and potential. Your knight is committed to the truth. His truth. He's focused. Driven. He'll do

running for it

anything to support his own agenda, but he doesn't have a strategy, and he can be rigid and inflexible."

"That doesn't sound like Ramsey at all," I couldn't help my sarcasm.

Luna met my gaze. "You can still influence things. You haven't lost control."

"But it's going to hurt." I'd heard everything she said.

"Probably. But you'll come out the other side better for it."

That other side was far enough away that I wasn't comforted.

Chapter Seventeen

Now that I was alone, I needed to think. Clear my head. I walked the few blocks to where Hunter was. Nothing had changed by the time I arrived; go figure.

As I approached I saw Hunter at the back of the dining room, on his phone, tablet set up in front of him. Was it wrong to be jealous that he'd found time to work? Maybe I should be grateful I'd married such an efficient man.

I wanted to roll my eyes at myself.

When I walked inside, he looked up. Like I'd flipped a switch, he set his phone down, and packed up his things as I approached. When I reached the table, he was on his feet, greeting me with a warm *Hey,* and a long, sweet kiss that was a heartbeat too long and too short both at the same time.

"I thought you were going to call me." He still sounded like the Hunter I knew. Kind. Polite.

"I needed to think."

"Did it help?"

I shook my head.

running for it

"Do you want coffee? Anything." He asked.

"No. That's the last thing I need." This was going to take some getting used to. Not his behavior—he wasn't acting much differently than I was used to—but my mind asking how I was supposed to act, with every single exchange. It wasn't like there were cameras in here. We weren't on display. But, best to get in the habit now.

"But if you have things to do, I can..." wait? I had a schedule to keep as well. "Have Luna drop me off." Was that the right response?

"Nope. I'm good to go." He wove his fingers through mine.

Holding hands as we walked out to his car was the most awkward thing we'd done so far. He was the gentleman I expected, opening the passenger door for me and making sure I was settled before hurrying to the driver's side.

As he sat, he didn't start the engine.

"Are you sure you don't have more to do?" I asked, hating that this disrupted two afternoons.

"I cleared the rest of my day for you, sweetie."

I winced at the awkward pet name.

Hunter furrowed his brow. "Babe?"

"That's a hard *no*."

He screwed his face up in thought. "My little flower blossom of sticky sweetness."

My laugh slipped out on its own. That felt nice. "Definitely not. Violet is fine."

"Violet it is." Hunter grasped my fingers to kiss the tips, then started the car and pulled us into traffic.

"You can just drop me off at my place," I said. "I have to do a few things before I pack, so I'll take my car. Meet you at your condo later."

"I really did clear my day. I'll go with you."

"I'm not going to run away."

Hunter smiled. "Hadn't considered it for a moment. But the longer you leave me alone with my thoughts, the bigger I realize the rock and hard place are that we're stuck between."

"Same."

"Settled." He navigated afternoon traffic with ease. "Where to first?"

"I need to stop by the shelter and tell the kids to pack, so they can move into the temporary place."

He turned down the next street that took us in that direction. "Done."

I didn't have the strength to argue the escort, and I didn't mind his company, so I settled in for the ride.

When we reached the shelter, I worked for several minutes to gather the kids, and was met with one *give me a minute* after another. I didn't want to let my impatience show, but my brain was ticking and I couldn't help but fidget.

running for it

Hunter squeezed my hand. "I've got this." He stuck two fingers in his mouth, and let out an ear-splitting whistle that the neighbors probably heard.

Impressive.

The sound of footsteps echoed back, all rushing toward us, accompanied by several people asking, "What was that?"

Double impressive.

"Is this everyone who's home?" I asked when most of them were gathered. There were only a couple of kids not here.

I was met with nods, but gazes were fixed on Hunter. Time to get this over with. "All right, here's the deal. We need to have some major remodeling done, and you're all going to a new place for just a little bit, while that happens. If you pack up, the bus will—"

"Is this the new ball and chain?" Someone asked

Another voice chimed in. "He's cute for a shackle."

Order was gone.

"Why haven't we met him before?"

"He's famous, right?"

"Does he know any basketball players?"

"Movie stars?"

"Is he good in bed?"

"Hey, Violet, my gaydar is going nuts over your new husband."

A fist squeezed my lungs, and I fought to breathe. I couldn't lie to these kids. "Pack your stuff." My words came out sharper than I intended. "This is all personal." I tried to soften my tone. "You can talk to any of the other volunteers if you have questions. I'll be right back."

I headed outside as fast as I could without looking like I was running.

"Violet." Hunter's voice hit my back.

I couldn't stop. I couldn't breathe. I couldn't—

He grabbed my arm and spun me.

I tried to gulp in the air, but it didn't work. Was this a panic attack? I was going to pass out. What the fuck was I doing?

"Hey." Hunter cupped my cheeks and forced my gaze to his. "Focus on me. Nothing else."

"That's the problem, isn't it?" My reply was shrill. "The focus is on you. Nothing else."

He didn't flinch. "Focus on my face. My voice. Climb out of your head, and live out here for a few."

I did what he said, pouring my attention toward his touch. His calm presence. "I can't do this." I managed to keep my voice steady. "I can't lie to those kids—to everyone. Nothing personal toward you."

running for it

"I get it." Hunter studied me. "Do you want me to call a lawyer? We'll tell everyone the truth right now."

If we did that, he'd have to deal with the fallout. Letting Ramsey down. His parents.

"What about... everything?" I floundered for a better word. If I backed out, I let him down, and I reneged on a promise. That was at least as bad as what we were doing now. "Why isn't there a third way to do this?"

"Maybe there is."

"How?"

"If there's one thing dating Ramsey taught me, it was how to keep a relationship private. We don't have to do this in front of the cameras. If you want a third option, an in-between point, that's it. We do this, but privately."

I couldn't see it. "You live a public life."

"*Ramsey* lives a public life. Most of our day-to-day isn't together. You and I will be the same."

But that wasn't the problem. "I don't give a fuck what the public thinks. What about the people we care about? Your parents will want to meet me. Lyn's throwing us a surprise party—surprise by the way, you didn't hear that from me."

"Do you want out?" Hunter's question was sincere, free of any accusation.

That *people we care about* included him. If ended things now, I definitely let him down now. If I didn't, I let other people down later. "I don't know."

"Then work with me to sort out the cleanest way possible to do this."

"Yeah." Did I have a choice? I was a slave to my own sense of responsibility.

I shut off my mind as best I could, to muddle my way through the rest of the conversation at the shelter, then through packing some essentials at my apartment. At Hunter's condo, he showed me the guest room. Told me the place was as much mine now as his, and to make myself comfortable.

I didn't see that happening, but that would be the case anywhere I went, not just here. Since I wasn't ready to unpack, I spent the next several hours doing shelter work. Calling contractors, getting estimates, making sure payments would clear until the money from these two fundraisers hit the accounts.

When Hunter knocked on my open door , my eyes were dry and my neck ached from me sitting on the bed to work, but I'd managed to forget the world for a while.

Now it was back.

"I'm going to pick up dinner," he said. "What're you in the mood for?"

running for it

My stomach grumbled at his question. Had I eaten today? "A lot of anything? Whatever you're in the mood for." I climbed from the bed to find my purse and give him cash.

"I was thinking burgers. And it's on me."

Yup, I was definitely hungry. And not letting him carry me. I handed him a twenty.

He refused to take it. "Let me. I'm not asking. I'll be back in a little bit."

"But—"

Hunter turned away.

Rude. I sank onto the edge of the bed as the front door opened and closed. Now what? I'd lost the groove I was in, and now my mind had time to wander.

"Hey." Ramsey stepped into view.

Or not. Every circuit in my brain shut off, leaving me with no idea of what to think or feel. "Hey."

"Hunter said you're having a hard time." He crossed the room to stop a short distance from me.

"Do I assume anything I say to him, you'll hear?" The question came out more sharply than I intended. "It's been a long day."

Ramsey sat next to me, and his leg pressed against mine. "He didn't tell me what you said, just that you were struggling. He's worried, and so am I.

I think I'm allowed concern, as your boyfriend." His tone was light.

It still weighed heavily on me. "I'm coping."

"I know what you're—"

"You don't have any idea what I'm going through. Lying to people is your life."

There was no response. I glanced sideways to see him frowning.

"I'm sorry." I hadn't meant my words to be so harsh.

"No. You're right. There are maybe three people in the world who I let see me. What else am I supposed to do?" Ramsey asked.

"You could stop pretending in front of everyone else."

"It's not that easy."

I wanted it to be. There were few things I wanted more than for Ramsey to be able to bury the mask. "What would happen if you did? If you came clean about everything? Or even just some of it? About Hunter." About me.

"My career would be over."

I couldn't deny that was a likely outcome. "If you keep on this path, the persona becomes the rest of your life. You're city council now, and you're already hiding something big. State senate is only a step or two from DC. Any secrets you have at that

running for it

point, will have to be buried so deep they'll devour you."

More silence.

I sighed. "You're tired of hearing me say it, and I'm tired of saying it."

"I'm scared." His voice was so soft, I wasn't sure I heard him right.

I wasn't going to ruin the moment by asking him to repeat himself. I held my breath, not wanting to miss what came next.

"This is who I am," Ramsey said.

"Not to me. Not to Hunter."

"This is what I've worked for. It's the thing I know. It's how I make a difference in the world."

"If you want to help, what you did in Vegas? That's help. Not empty promises you may or may not be able to keep, but bringing funds and positive attention to places that need it."

He shook his head. "But that's not where I am right now."

My shoulders slumped. Here we were again, in the same place as when we'd broken up. There was less yelling this time, and I was more willing to admit it was going to hurt like hell to lose Ramsey. But it had been a day, and I was already cracking. "What I told you in Vegas, that if you ask me to do this…"

"That it's over for us." He sounded resigned.

"And I know I made this choice. I'm here because I said I would be, and I'll see things through with Hunter. But…" My throat ached. I didn't want to reach for the next words. Thinking them, vocalizing them, would make them real.

Ramsey twisted on the mattress and placed a finger under my chin. "I love you." Sincerity bled from his words.

And it almost tore my heart apart. Of course the bastard would pick now to say that. "I love you too." So much. "But the life you live? I can't. I can't sign on for years or even months more of lies. Even when the wedding issue is fixed, there are still more. Will you keep pretending you're single? Finally come out? Tell the world you're with one of us and ask the other to hide? I can't do that. Hunter deserves better that that. I don't have a problem with you seeing both of us, but the secrets? I can't be a part of that."

"I'm not going to stop trying to make things right."

I shook my head. "Only one thing makes this right."

"There has to be a compromise, and I'm stubborn." Ramsey dropped his hands to my hips and tugged me toward him.

I clenched my jaw. "You think now is the time for sex?"

"No. But let me hold you for a little while."

running for it

I wanted to push him away, but I also wanted to climb into his lap and never leave. I leaned into him and pulled his arms around me. I wanted to cry, but the tears weren't there. Why did this have to hurt so much?

Chapter Eighteen

Getting up early, so I could open the cafe, was the most familiar and normal thing I'd done in days. Stumbling bleary-eyed through unfamiliar rooms, and a shower… not so much.

My plan was simple. I'd be out of here and on my way to work before Hunter woke up, and I'd send him a text letting him know I'd be home late, which would happen even if I weren't avoiding him. No need to for awkward conversation. For pretending I didn't ache over my break-up with Ramsey last night.

The pit in Hunter's eyes last night, when I told him why I'd rather eat somewhere they weren't, had been bad enough.

I liked plans, and this one was straightforward.

Except I had to pass by the kitchen to get to the front door, and the light was already on.

"Coffee?" Hunter asked.

I steeled myself—now was a good time to practice for the rest of the day—and turned to find him leaning against the far kitchen counter, next to

running for it

the coffee maker. "I'll grab coffee at work." My tone was light and pleasant.

"You doing okay?" he asked.

"I'm good." I was so, so not good.

"No. Really. How are you?"

I sighed. "We're not performing for anyone in here; you don't have to do this."

He raised an eyebrow. "Are you talking to me, or yourself? You know I genuinely care."

"I do. I just…" Another sigh. I'd have to get that under control too. "I'm running on determination and if I stop, I'll stall."

"You have to process."

I leaned against the door with my arms crossed, more to hold myself in than to keep him out. "If I do, I'll crumble. I won't be able to stop fixating on how fucked up this all is."

"All right." Hunter sounded as unhappy with the conversation as I felt. He grabbed a travel mug from the counter next to him. "Take the coffee anyway? I don't drink mine the same way you do, and it would be a shame to dump this." He crossed the room to hand me the stainless steel.

Warmth sparked in my stomach, and a resigned smile slipped out. I took the mug from him. "All right. Thank you. By the way, I'll be home pretty late tonight."

"Is it something I said?" His laugh was weak.

"No. I promise. Even if I weren't here, doing"—I waved my free hand in lieu of words—"I'd have to work late. After Lyn's, I have a bunch of shelter work to do, and it's easier from there."

"That's fair. Be safe."

I nodded. It felt odd walking out the door. It wasn't like I was going to give him a goodbye kiss or anything, though.

When I got to work, I found Lyn in the kitchen, as was typical in the mornings. She'd already been up for hours, baking for the day. She looked surprised to see me. "I kind of hoped you'd call in, and take me up on that offer for time off."

"Do you even know me?" It was a struggle to keep my teasing from sounding forced.

Lyn arranged croissants in a neat row in a wire display basket. "You just got married."

Right. "And we're planning something big"— it wasn't really a lie, the big thing was just more like *divorce* than *honeymoon*—"but he has obligations, I have things I can't let slide. Trust me, things are still intense at home." Suffocatingly.

Lyn handed me the basket. "Hunter always struck me as a good guy."

"He really is wonderful." The truth was so much easier than bullshit. "I'm gonna prep to open." I walked back into the main shop, placed the croissants on display behind glass, and got to work.

running for it

The rest of the day was long, but uneventful, and I was worn out when I got *home* that night. The small lamp left on in the living room, even though Hunter had gone to bed, made me smile. I shut everything off, and as I climbed into bed, I let exhaustion take over my mind.

The next morning, Hunter was up and waiting, with coffee, when I got to the kitchen. I wanted to tell him he didn't have to do this for me, but when I'd dated Ramsey—my heart ached at the name—Hunter had always been up this early.

"Still a morning person?" I asked lightly. "And thank you." I took the coffee he handed me and sipped cautiously. Perfect temperature.

"I am until someone makes me stop. And, sorry to get all business on you first thing in the morning…"

My sliver of disappointment wanted a friendly, no-pressure chat, but *business* was probably better. "It's fine."

"Will you be home for dinner tonight?"

"Is there something on the calendar? Are we expecting guests?" I hadn't been told and forgotten. Had I? Dinner with his mother was tomorrow night, but I'd set aside time to dread that after work.

"The question is exactly what it is." Hunter almost looked amused. "If you're going to be here, I'll plan on enjoying your company."

Oh. There was that spark of warmth again, bigger this time. "That sounds nice. I'll be here."

My mood was lighter than in a few days—charcoal instead of pitch black, but I'd take it—as I headed to work. Once there, things ran the way they should. The way they always had. It was soothing to fall into the familiar routine, including my weekly, mid-morning meeting with Lyn to talk schedules and ordering, and just check in.

Elle, one of the bakers Lyn had finally hired as backup, on Owen's insistence, poked her head into Lyn's office. "Ramsey is here for you."

His visiting wasn't unusual—though the knot that formed in my stomach at his name was tighter than I was used to. He was a fan of the chocolate croissants, and stopped by a lot to chat with Lyn.

She looked at me as she stood. "Do you want to hide back here? I don't know how things are with—"

"Sorry, no," Elle said. "He's here for Violet."

My blood ran hot and cold at the same time. Pretty sure that wasn't good for me.

"I can tell him you're busy." Lyn looked concerned.

So, so tempting. I stood anyway. "It's okay. I've got this." When I saw him, the way my feet threatened to stop without my permission, maybe I didn't have it after all. A pang of hurt and longing

running for it

gripped me. When we'd gotten back together, I had a fantasy I hadn't dared vocalize even to myself. That if he and I made things right, if we were back together, when he came in here he'd greet me with a long kiss, and no one would bat an eye.

That wasn't happening.

His smile was a poor substitute for more, but I'd take it. I stopped close enough to be polite, but far enough to try to keep temptation at bay.

"Hey." His greeting was as casual as his posture.

Fucking bastard. Would it be worse if he could hide how this was impacting him, or if his stance was genuine. No, I knew better. He missed me too. "Hey." I couldn't fake it as well as he did.

"Can we talk someplace?"

Out here is fine. That was what I wanted to say, so I wasn't sure why, "The storeroom?" came out instead.

He nodded, and followed me. The room was barely big enough for two rows of shelves, and freezer against the back wall. I had no idea why I locked the door behind us.

Ramsey raised an eyebrow. "If this is your office, I need to talk to Lyn about giving you an upgrade." His tone was light.

"What, you don't like the place?" I swept my arm to gesture to everything. "I decorated it myself.

And I have fast access to the chocolate stash." I patted the freezer.

"I *am* a little jealous of that. I— Oh my God." Ramsey's gaze stalled on the top of the shelf dividing the room. "Is that the new Wing Zero Custom?"

So freaking adorkable. Damn it. "They came in a week ago. Lyn was supposed to tell you. I asked her to make sure she got you an extra one when she placed her order." I sat on the freezer. This should keep some distance between us.

He stepped closer, between my legs, and settled his hands on my knees. "You're sexy when you feed my Gunpla fascination."

My entire body lit up like a Christmas tree, and my heart hammered against my ribs. It would be so easy to say I didn't mean the other night. To take it all back. He'd accept that. "I'm a married woman now." My retort came out far flirtier than I intended.

"To my boyfriend. And your husband knows I'm here." Ramsey slipped even closer.

The conversation with Luna popped into my head, maybe as a way to distract me from Ramsey, or simply my brain's screwed up sense of humor. "Do you remember when Luna was arrested."

"You're kidding, right?"

Fair point. "She says someone pulled strings to get her a reduced sentence. She told me that yesterday. Do you know anything about that?"

running for it

Ramsey twisted his mouth. "Should I?"

"She thinks it was you. Was it?"

There was a long pause before Ramsey said "Yes."

"Why didn't you ever tell me?"

"I did it because it was the right thing to do. Luna didn't deserve that situation and I could help. I didn't tell you because I didn't want you to feel obligated for… anything."

"Thank you. A few years late, but thank you." I poured the sincerity into my words. While secrets were status quo for Ramsey, he loved recognition as much as he did anything. It must have devoured him to keep this to himself.

"Now that we have that out of the way…" His voice was low, with a hint of growl underneath. He tilted closer, angling his mouth toward mine. "I miss you, Taffy."

I swore my heart paused. It took all of my willpower to plant my palm on his chest and stop him. "Nothing's changed."

He sighed and straightened, but didn't move away. "How are you?"

"Fine."

"No, really."

"Perfectly all right. I'm still keeping everyone's secrets."

He traced his thumb along the seam of my jeans, near my knee. Did he know he was doing it? "This is me you're talking to. No secrets in here, and I'm worried about you."

"Did you bring me a solution that doesn't force you and Hunter out before he's ready? That doesn't hurt anyone we know?"

"I'm working on something, and those aren't just words. But everything I've come up with so far is going to hurt Hunter."

Aside from stepping out of the spotlight and letting us end things quietly. But that wasn't Ramsey, and it never would be. I was okay with that, until the fakeness came into play.

His hands inched higher on my thighs. "Ravyn stopped by my office to tell me she knows this entire wedding thing is bullshit."

"That sounds like her." I let a tiny smile slip out.

"Kingston keeps asking if I'm all right with losing you."

Odd. I barely knew Kingston, and really only through Lyn. He hadn't lived here when Ramsey and I dated, so the first time I met him and Owen was when they tried to buy Lyn's shop. "Why would he think you aren't?"

"Because he's heard me talk about you." Ramsey made it sound like the most obvious answer in the world.

running for it

"Ramsey…" I was short on protests or the desire to use them, but I needed to.

"I know. It still doesn't change anything." His hands were on my hips now. "I had to see you today. I had to tell you…" He sighed and pressed his forehead to mine.

I couldn't pull way, and I struggled to find my voice. "Tell me what?"

"Everything. So much more than I can put into words."

Like the other night, when I'd told him we were done, I didn't want to pull away. "I have to get back to work." Such a simple phrase for something that was so hard to say.

Ramsey let go and stepped back. "Yeah. I'll see you around."

I sat on the freezer for who knows how long after he left. It didn't help me collect my thoughts any. I finally hopped to the floor and tracked Lyn down in her office to finish our meeting.

"Close the door," she said.

Odd request, but I did and settled into the seat across from her desk.

"Do you remember the remodel?' Lyn flipped her pen between her fingers. She was staring at her computer.

"The one where you gutted half the store and expanded? Vaguely."

"And that I had cameras installed almost everywhere except the kitchen, for insurance reasons."

"Of cour— Oh." Reality slammed into me. Including cameras in the storeroom.

Lyn frowned. "Yeah. Oh."

She'd seen me cuddled with Ramsey. "It's not… I mean… Hunter knows." I was so bad at keeping these secrets.

"It's not my place to tell you how to live." Lyn's expression softened. "To say what kind of relationships you should or shouldn't have. As long as all of you are on the same page, I don't have to worry about who I let down by either telling or keeping the secret."

I didn't know what to say, and I hated that.

"You're not just an employee, you're a friend," Lyn said. "I want you to be all right."

"Me too."

"As all right as those people around you."

I clamped my jaw shut again. It was a convoluted way to say it, but she didn't understand, the people around me came first. I wasn't ready to get into that argument with Lyn.

She tapped her pen against the desk. "I don't bring up that I saw you two to make things weird. It's a warning. If you're hiding something, and I found out in just a few days, other people will too."

running for it

"I know."

"Do you? Owen and Kingston work hard for their anonymity, and it *is* work. Ramsey. Well…"

Ramsey was exactly the opposite.

"Trust me, I'm very aware." But this drove home the point.

Chapter Nineteen

I actually slept Saturday night, though it was more a collapse of exhaustion than it was a peaceful thing. I woke up early Sunday, despite not having to open the café, and I was grateful to leave half-formed dreams behind of letting everyone around me down. Of our worlds crumbling when the truth came out.

I sleepwalked my way through a shower and dressing. My schedule was busy, even with the day off from one job. The first contractor was coming by the shelter today to start ripping out carpets and any Sheetrock with mold damage.

Hunter was in the kitchen already. I shouldn't be surprised at this point.

"I'm not interrupting your morning moments of peace, am I?" I rarely had enough time in the morning to stop and enjoy the solitude, but when I did, I wanted solitude.

"Not at all." He slid a mug of coffee and a bowl of oatmeal across the counter. "I heard you in the shower, so I made extra breakfast."

running for it

I had to admit, the best part of being married to Hunter was that it was Hunter. I settled on a kitchen stool. "If you're not careful, I'll get used to this. You're spoiling me."

"Nothing wrong with that." His smile was easy. Calming. Didn't reach his eyes.

I stalled with a spoonful of oatmeal halfway to my mouth. "What's wrong?"

"Trying to decide when it's best to break the news."

I dropped my spoon and it clattered against the edge of the bowl. Fortunately it didn't send oatmeal flying, but I wasn't sure that was a priority. "Probably best to just tell me at this point."

"I talked to Mom a few hours ago. They've asked her to stay another month, and she wasn't able to get through until now to tell me. She can't make dinner tonight."

Relief flooded me. "I'm… sorry?"

"No you're not."

At least I was consistent and obvious. "I'm sorry it seems to have you upset."

"I'm ambivalent. I didn't want to look her in the eye and play this game, but whenever she stays out longer than planned, I worry about her. She pushes too hard for others sometimes—she's a lot like you."

Except I'd never ask my child—only son or not—to lie to their other parent about their sexuality, simply to keep the peace. "Hmm."

"Don't judge." An edge slipped into Hunter's voice.

"I didn't say anything."

"You think very loudly sometimes."

I didn't have a response so I shoved some rapidly cooling oatmeal into my mouth instead. But it wasn't really a lot to chew around, so the bite didn't take long. The mood in the room had cooled too, so I might as well ask what I was thinking. "When we do have dinner with her, are we really going to sit through an entire meal and lie to her? What happens when this ends? Will you and Ramsey hide things forever? How will she feel when she finds out otherwise?"

"I don't know. I don't have any more answers than you."

Silence settled between us. It wasn't awkward, but I still had a desire to fill it with anything to keep my mind from tripping over all the *what if* scenarios it was coming up with. Problem was, those same topics were the only ones I could think of.

I thanked Hunter for breakfast and headed to the shelter. Deconstruction turned to scheduling more appointments, turned to making the budget work with fresh damage found under the carpet.

running for it

When my phone buzzed with a new text, I realized it was after eight at night. No wonder my eyes were dry and my neck ached.

You all right? The message was from Hunter.

New guilt. I should be much better at processing it, based on the last week. *I'm fine. Just lost track of time. I'm sorry if I made you worry.*

It's okay, as long as you are.

I am, I wrote. *I'm not sure when I'll be home, though.* It was both nice and a new kind of stress having someone at home waiting for me.

I got home a little before midnight. Tomorrow was going to be a long day. Hunter's bedroom door was closed, but he'd left a lamp on for me in the living room.

Sleep sucked that night, and I didn't hit that sweet, deep-slumber part until right before my alarm went off. I hit *snooze* far more times than I should have, and panic mingled with the lingering traces of bad dreams as I got ready.

As I was stepping into the shower, my reflection caught my attention and I spun. The person who stared back had dark circles under a glare of accusation. The Violet in the mirror almost screamed with accusation.

I shoved the self-loathing down and finished as quickly as I could.

Hunter was in the kitchen—at least something was pleasant about my morning. "I wasn't sure if I should wake you." His voice was kind. "This will have to do instead." He handed me a coffee to go.

The simple kindness clawed at my throat and tears pricked my eyes. Was I really getting emotional over coffee? I forced a smile. "Thank you."

"I can tell it's a bad time to ask, but you'll be more upset if I don't."

My insides clenched. "What's up?"

"Are you still up for the fundraiser tonight?"

I forced out a laugh, but I couldn't believe I'd forgotten. The reminder was in my calendar that I hadn't had time to check this morning, and I hated that the event slipped my mind. Those stupid, useless tears were threatening again. Goddess, I needed sleep.

"Of course." I smiled too brightly. Faking it for strangers would be a lot easier than with our friends.

I made it through the day thanks to heavy doses of caffeine and sugar, but I was ready to crash when I got home. It would have to wait. A new dress hung on the back of my bedroom door. Nothing as elegant as I'd worn in Vegas, but it was still stunning.

If I were less tired, I might be amused that Hunter and Ramsey were better at picking dresses for me than I was.

running for it

Events like this—fundraisers for whatever candidate Ramsey or his family was schmoozing at the time—had always been my least favorite part of dating him.

I doubted that being at one tonight, watching him from across the room as he smiled and laughed and flitted from person to person, would make the evening any better.

The instant we stepped from the car in front of the country club, even as the valet was pulling away, Hunter was by my side, offering his arm. I hooked my hand in the crook of his elbow, and he covered it with a long, tender kiss on the lips.

It may have been for show, but it felt natural.

When we stepped inside, Ramsey was the first person I spotted. The way Hunter's hand tightened over mine, I suspected I wasn't the only one. He leaned in close, mouth near my ear. "You got this?"

I nodded, fake smile in place as if he'd just whispered the sweetest thing.

So many people congratulated us that I lost count. I smiled through every guy with a version of *you got yourself a real looker* and every woman saying *so sad you're off the market now* imaginable.

As soon as anyone turned away, it was a different story. I'd learned a long time ago that listening to the background chatter at these things was toxic at best. Tonight it was impossible to ignore the murmurs.

Do you think it's real?

It won't last.

I always thought Hunter Sorenson was… you know.

I was tempted on several occasions to pull away and tell people exactly what I thought of their gossip. But Hunter's subtle grip kept me in place, and reminded me at the same time I wasn't alone in this.

Seeing Ramsey was still the hardest though. His handshake for Hunter and kiss on the cheek for me were the most fake things ever, and he made both look more genuine than anyone else here.

Then Ramsey was swept away again. Each time he tried to approach us the rest of the night, someone stepped in his path.

Turned out I still hated these parties.

The ride home was quiet. I didn't know if Hunter was respecting my exhaustion or if he was as conflicted about the evening as me.

When we stepped inside, I muttered, "Good night," and turned toward my room. Being so close to security, to solitude, was shattering the walls I'd had up all day. The reinforcements I'd put in place for this evening had already splintered.

"Violet." Hunter's voice was weak.

running for it

I couldn't. I walked into my room without looking back. With the door closing me off from the world, everything inside me crumbled. Everything I needed to do, everyone I needed to help, look out for, lie for, all pressed in on me until I couldn't breathe.

I stripped off my dress, and grabbed a nightshirt.

The fist around my chest clenched tighter.

I sank to the edge of my bed before my legs could give out. The thigh-high stockings and lacy underwear weren't me. Not like this. What was I doing?

Tears stung my eyelids, and I scrubbed them away with the back of my hand. I tugged on my shirt. Yanked off the first stocking.

A sob tore from my throat, and it loosed the tears I was fighting. And then I was wailing and gasping for air.

"Violet?" Hunter pounded on my door.

I bit the side of my fist to muffle myself, but I couldn't stop crying.

"I'm coming in," Hunter said and walked into the room. He sat next to me on the bed, and wrapped his arms around me. The comfort was perfect, which made me cry harder.

He was the one thing about this entire situation that didn't suck, and getting away from him was the one thing that was going to make it better.

He didn't ask what was wrong. Not that I could have paused long enough to answer. He simply held me until the tears were dried up, and my throat was raw and my eyes ached.

At some point, he tucked me in, but I didn't want him to leave. I grabbed his arm and tugged him next to me under the covers. I don't know when or how I fell asleep, but when I woke up Hunter was still wrapped around me, protecting me.

I opened my eyes to find him watching me.

His eyes crinkled at the corners when he smiled. "I promise I'm not staring at you while you sleep, like a creeper. I just woke up."

"You say that…" I wasn't in the mood to laugh, the weight of everything hadn't lifted while I slept, but he was making me feel better. "Think we've found the latest sleep fashions?" I gestured down to me in my T-shirt and single stocking and him in a button-down with boxers.

"Something tells me Paris won't be knocking down our door."

"They're missing out."

Hunter brushed a strand of hair from my forehead. "Do you want to talk about it?"

"I really don't have anything new to say." I was sick of sounding like a broken record every time I spouted off *we need to fix things*, and nothing was going to get better if the situation stayed the same.

Chapter Twenty

It was easier to let the days blend into each other, to run on auto-pilot, than to let my mind wander. If I focused on the tasks I had to do—cafe, shelter, home, repeat, I could get everything done that I needed to, without breaking.

As Thursday at the cafe wound to a close, concern set in. Tomorrow was supposed to be a cafe day off, but Lyn had asked me to come in for a few hours in the afternoon to help with inventory. I'd been torn between jumping at the chance to stay busy, and the fact that I hadn't had time to go visit the kids from the shelter all week. The other volunteers were available in the new place, but I missed the kids.

Keeping distracted and helping Lyn had won out.

When I got back to Hunter's and stepped inside, he and Ramsey were on the couch, sitting close heads bowed together.

They both looked up at the same time.

I hated that I'd interrupted whatever they were doing. I hated even more than seeing Ramsey ached so much.

"I didn't mean to interrupt," I said quickly, before either of them could pick the direction of the conversation. "I'll be in my room."

"You don't have to scurry away. It's your house too." Hunter was kind.

But it wasn't really.

"Stay, Taffy." Ramsey managed sweetness and command perfectly with those two words.

And I couldn't do it. Not here. Not where I was should be able to let down my guard and relax for at least a little while. "Why? So Hunter and I can practice being the perfect couple for an audience? Do you want to make sure we're cuddling and kissing properly?" The words fell with more exhaustion than venom.

A shadow passed over Ramsey's face. "I really don't. Not when I'm not a part of it."

"Stay, please." Hunter's request stopped me from tumbling down the rabbit hole of examining Ramsey's response. "Keep us company. You're not intruding."

The longer I lingered in this room, the harder it was to make my feet carry me away. I wanted to spend time with them. I'd been enjoying Hunter's company, and I'd never been good at turning away

running for it

from Ramsey. Even the fact that I'd ended things with him before we ever really restarted didn't make it any easier to ignore how I felt.

"All right." It was easier to say than I wanted it to be. I headed toward the chair next to them.

Hunter stood. "I'll grab you a drink." He approached me and planted his hands on my hips to make sure we didn't collide. The assisted side-step put me closer to Ramsey, who wrapped an arm around my waist and pulled me to sit on the couch next to him.

The entire thing happened so fast I barely caught every step. I let out an amused huff. "I'd be upset that the two of you just handed me off like a football, if that hadn't been the smoothest thing ever."

"That's the point," Ramsey said.

I rolled my eyes, but I wasn't interested in relocating. It was comfortable next to him.

Hunter returned quickly, and handed me a glass with ice and orange juice.

I didn't know anyone who drank juice this way, especially at night, but it was exactly what I was in the mood for. "Thank you." I took a drink, and set the glass on the coaster Hunter had provided. "I really didn't mean to interrupt."

"You aren't," Ramsey assured me. "In fact, we were just talking about you."

"That makes me nervous."

Hunter shook his head. "Because Ramsey's being an asshole with his phrasing. Remember the first time you and I met?"

There was no way I could forget that. "I thought I was going to die of embarrassment." It was when I started dating Ramsey. Hunter was supposedly gone for the weekend, so Ramsey and I were fucking in the living room of their apartment. Hunter had canceled his plans, and walked in on us.

"Nothing to be embarrassed about." Hunter settled on my other side, sitting sideways so his shin rested against my thigh and he faced us both.

"I'm not now." Not with Hunter. I couldn't even say when it became as easy for me to be nude—more—around Hunter as it was around Ramsey, but I had no issues with it now. "I was then. Why were you talking about me?"

"I was so happy to finally meet the elusive *Taffy*. The instant I saw you, I knew I was right about you being good for Ramsey."

Ramsey shifted forward, to perch on the edge of his seat. "You never told me that."

"Was it my ass or tits that helped you draw that conclusion?" I was teasing, but given those were probably the first parts of me Hunter had seen, I was curious.

running for it

Hunter smiled. "It was the fact that you were in our apartment. You were the first partner he'd brought home in more than three years of living together."

"Oh." Realization sank in. When I'd met Ramsey, he hadn't even given me his real name the first night. It didn't take me long to figure it out it was because *Ramsey Miller* was as much a brand as a name, and he planned to be a much bigger one going forward, and the last thing he needed was to earn a reputation as a guy who had a propensity toward orgies. "But you said… you'd already drawn conclusions about me. What first made you think I'd be good for him?"

"When he washed that shitty black dye out of his hair." Hunter winked.

"*Hey*." Ramsey was indignant. "I'm a sexy fucking brunette."

"You're sexy. Period," Hunter said. "As a brunette… you're just trying too hard."

I liked the playful exchange. The honesty was a welcome relief and the ease of the banter was familiar and comforting. "I've always been partial to your natural auburn," I said to Ramsey.

"He lightens it because blond polls better."

"*Ha*." I wasn't surprised by Hunter's confession. "I so called that."

Ramsey clenched his jaw, but amusement danced in his eyes. "Not sure I like being ganged up on this way."

"Violet never complains about being double teamed."

I flushed at Hunter's words. "Not once. I think you might like it if you give it a try, Lollie." That was the name Ramsey gave me the night we met. He'd also given me a horrible pick-up line to go with it. I hadn't called him that since, but tonight it seemed appropriate.

Ramsey's growl was almost primal, and in a flash he straddled my legs and pinned my wrists to the cushion on either side of me. "I think I'm happier being on top." He was as much playfulness as threat.

"You sure?" I teased. "Because that's the perfect position for Hunter to ride your ass."

Ramsey raised an eyebrow. "You'd like that, wouldn't you?"

Now that the images were in my head, both men naked, the groans each of them made when they were turned on, and Hunter entering Ramsey from behind... Desire pulsed between my legs. "Yeah, actually."

"I don't top." Hunter nudged Ramsey's shoulder.

running for it

Ramsey let me go and rolled back into his own seat, landing with a chuckle. "Life is a lot better with all three of us."

Such a simple statement, but it threatened to send me into a spiral of regret and doubt. I didn't want that.

"Remember that weekend at Timpanogos?" Hunter's question kept me here.

I was happy to linger in the pleasant memories. "When you made me watch the entire *08th MS Team* series?"

"*Made* you?" Ramsey laughed. "What we *made* was your world a brighter place, for the experience."

I couldn't argue that, but it had more to do with the company than the show. "It's idealistic."

"Your face is idealistic," Hunter said.

"*Gee, Ramsey.*" He'd summoned that fake-Violet voice. "*Thank you for improving my life forever with Gundam.*"

This was so ridiculous. And twice as fun. "I've got much better curves than a Zaku."

Hunter shook his head. "No one has more perfect curves than a Zaku." He managed to say it with a straight face.

"They're perfectly symmetrical. Fantastic for engineering," Ramsey agreed. "But I prefer my people with a little softness."

I looked between them with disbelief. "I can't believe you're comparing me to a giant robot. And they're not even the good guys."

"But you still come out on top," Ramsey said as if it were obvious.

I couldn't help but take the conversation back a few minutes. "Unlike Hunter."

"Nice." Hunter laughed.

"At the time you said you enjoyed the show." Ramsey was still in serious mode.

I had a counter he'd appreciate. "Iron Blooded Orphans is a far more poignant moral examination of war."

Ramsey stared at me in surprise. "We never watched that with you."

"You watched without us." Hunter sounded just as shocked.

"All of it. Every single thing Gundam I could find, translated or not." I'd also made sure my favorites were available for the shelter.

Ramsey's smirk was all self-satisfaction. "We converted you."

But that spiral of sadness was back without my permission. Tugging my heart and weighing me down. "I watch them because they remind me of you." I wanted to sound light and playful, but reality was back, slamming into my heart. "I don't want to be without you." But I couldn't be with him—

running for it

them—either. I couldn't finish the thought out loud. "I'm gonna head to bed."

Ramsey grabbed my wrist. "Taffy."

I jerked out of his grip, unable to look at him.

"Violet?" Hunter was softer.

I couldn't do this. I walked away.

Chapter Twenty-One

I bypassed the kitchen the next morning, and headed straight to the shelter without stopping to see Hunter. It wasn't that I didn't want to talk to him—it was the opposite. If I stopped and chatted, I'd remember the fun. I'd regret what wouldn't happen with Ramsey. I'd hate the reminder that this thing with Hunter wasn't real.

The last thought hit like a fist to the gut. It should have been an aftershock—no real impact—but I felt the sadness there as much as everywhere else.

Fortunately, there was more than enough work at the shelter to keep me busy. Administrative needs hadn't stopped for construction, and I had stacks of invoices, media requests, and messages for other various things to sift through.

My phone buzzed a little before lunch, and I grabbed it without looking up from my work. "This is Violet."

running for it

"Hey." Hunter's voice soothed me just like that, despite me not wanting it to. "Are you free for lunch?"

I could be. I shouldn't be. Did I almost miss the catch in his voice? "What's up?"

He sighed. "I got a call a little bit ago. From my dad. He's having a good health day, he heard the great news about his only son getting married, and he wants to meet my new wife."

"Oh." My insides twisted in on themselves. This was the last thing I wanted to do ever—look a dying man in the eye and lie to him about his son's relationships. "I have to work at the cafe this afternoon, but I can spare a little time." The words flowed out on their own. I'd stayed with Hunter because of this. It had to be done, no matter how much I dreaded it.

"When are you free?"

I wasn't getting anything else done until this meeting was over. "Now is good."

"I'll pick you up in about fifteen minutes. And Violet? Thank you." The genuine gratitude in Hunter's voice didn't erase my dread, but it did add a hint of sweet to the bitter taste in the back of my throat.

Since I was done working for now, I decided to wait outside for Hunter. The chill in the air sapped the heat from my cheeks, and I gulped in the fresh cold, trying to freeze my insides as well. When Hunter arrived, I hopped in the car almost before it stopped moving.

"Eager to get this over with?" he asked flatly.

Oh, there was more guilt. Wonderful. I couldn't lie, but the truth didn't seem right either, so I shrugged into my seatbelt.

"Me too." Hunter's voice was soft. He reached over and rested a hand on my knee, and the cold all rushed away.

We made the short trip in silence. The sign on the front door of the hospice facility said *Out of respect for our guests, please silence your phones.* I hated cutting myself off from the world, but it was polite, and we wouldn't be here long.

Inside the building looked more a high-end apartment complex than a medical facility. Rich wood paneling and plush carpet led us down a softly lit hallway, past widely spaced doors.

Hunter stopped in front of one and knocked. A voice that sounded so much like his called, "Come in."

We stepped into what would have been a large, nicely finished bedroom, if it weren't for all the monitors and wires surrounding a bed near the window. The man lying there, dwarfed by pillows and a heavy blanket, looked remarkably like Hunter. Older, with gray hair, and a bit frailer. But the face

running for it

was the same. The kindness in his dark eyes was the same. Even his smile was familiar.

It would be sweet if I didn't know this was the man Hunter was hiding a part of his identity for.

They exchanged a couple words of greeting, and Hunter gestured to me. "Dad, this is my wife, Violet. Violet, this is Hunter Sr."

"Call me Dad, hon." He reached for my hand when I offered it in greeting, and pressed it between his palms. His skin was yellow and papery, but his grip and smile were warm and friendly. "I remember you. You were with Ramsey Miller for a while."

At least things were going to get awkward right away. I had no idea how to response. "Yes."

"I see." Hunter Sr. shook his head. "You know, I always figured you and he split because he was in love with my son."

Hunter coughed.

"But I can tell you and Hunter care about each other," his dad said.

Hunter reached for my hand and squeezed gently. "We do."

The simple statement rang with a clarity I hadn't had much of lately. We really did. For so long I'd only thought of Hunter as *Ramsey's friend*, but he'd been here for me. Still was. I was as terrified of him being gone from my life as I was Ramsey.

Hunter's dad pushed himself into a sitting position in bed. "Violet, hon, you've always seemed like a lovely person, so please don't take this the wrong way—"

Was there any other way to take a statement that started like that?

"—The last few years have taught me that putting off conversations means you may never get to have them, and this is one I need to have with my son." He looked at Hunter. "What the fuck are you doing, Junior?"

Hunter's wide-eyed expression reflected my shock. He worked his jaw. "I don't—"

"Anyone with half a brain can see how you and Ramsey feel about each other. I hoped you'd tell me at some point."

What was happening? My brain was glitching on reality versus expectation.

Hunter didn't look to be doing any better. "I'm not—"

"Going to lie to me, are you? You'd never send your old man to meet his maker on a lie."

"No, I wouldn't." Hunter's shoulders drooped, but the corner of his mouth tugged up. "And you're right. I do love Ramsey. He feels the same." The confession slid out on a puff of tangible relief.

I wanted to cheer for Hunter for being able to say it, but I was still struggling to process the

running for it

unexpected situation. Would there be fallout from the confession? Screaming and name calling and accusations?

"I'm so proud of you." Hunter Sr opened his arms wide, and pulled Hunter into a warm hug.

Laughter and tears both bubbled up in my throat, spreading from the warm spot in my chest. The moment mingled with a flood of stories the shelter kids had told me. With memories of my sister. It was so beautiful in here, but so bittersweet.

"I'm sorry you found out this way, hon." Dad's voice was kind as he let Hunter go and focused on me. "It's best you know now, before you're with him too long."

I laughed through threatening tears and scrubbed my hand across my cheeks. He was apologizing to me?

"Did we break you?" Hunter Sr sounded concerned.

Hunter pulled me closer, and tangled his fingers with mine. "Probably just the opposite. Violet already knows how I feel."

His dad held up a finger, then snapped his mouth shut. "You know what? I don't want too many details there, as long as you're all on the same page. Why didn't you ever tell me? I've been waiting for you to *come out*, and then I hear you're married."

"Mom asked me—begged me—not to tell you. She said I couldn't send you to your grave knowing I was attracted to men. That it would hurt you so much."

"I raised you better than to think lies were the solution."

"You raised me to look good, and always have a woman on my arm. *Look at how handsome he is. He's going to break so many girls' hearts.* That's all I heard growing up."

There was an edge to Hunter's voice that I'd heard so many times.

His dad frowned. "You're right, and I'm sorry. Saying *I didn't know any better* doesn't change that, but it's the truth. I think I saw it when you were young, but I was scared. For me. For you. But everything you've done, I couldn't be more proud of you. As long as whomever you're with is treating you right, I don't care what's between their legs."

And now I wanted to cry again, and the acceptance in the room. "Thank you." I did mean to say the words aloud, and now two sets of eyes were on me. "If more kids could hear things like this…"

"What can I say? I'm incredible." Despite his frail appearance, he sounded as strong and confident as anyone I knew. "Whatever your reasons for doing this, Violet, thank you for being my son's friend."

running for it

"It goes both ways." It felt good to smile. To speak my mind. It felt *really* good. "And he's worth it."

"Come here." Hunter Sr gestured, and pulled me in for a tight hug. When he let me go, he did the same with Hunter, holding him for several seconds.

He pointed to a pair of chairs next to the bed. "Stay for a while. Catch me up. Introduce me to your *wife*. Tell me what's going on with you. With Ramsey."

This was the single most wholesome, warm moment I'd been a part of in a long time. As the three of us talked, the rest of the world slipped away. Dad had countless stories about Hunter. He was fantastic at bringing me into the conversation, too.

I loved every minute of it, not only for Hunter, but it was a reminder for me. Not every parent with a gay kid was an asshole. I wished my shelter kids, my sister, had this. It ached that they hadn't. But at the same time, the warmth that flowed between Hunter and his dad meant there were other families out there like theirs. With acceptance and love.

That filled me with hope.

As Hunter and I walked out of the hospice a few hours later, we were both smiling.

"I like your dad. He's—"

"Painfully direct and honest?" Hunter reached for his phone.

I did the same. "I wasn't thinking in those terms, but yes."

"He liked you too. He doesn't chat like that with just anyone." Hunter's bright smile wilted as he looked at his phone.

My *What's wrong* stuck in my throat as I saw a handful of missed calls and a texts, all from Lyn. "Shit." I'd blown through my start time for inventory. The nausea was back full force as I called Lyn back.

"Are you all right?" she answered, breathless.

Damn it. "I'm fine. I'm so sorry. We were talking to Hunter's father. I lost track of time. I'm so so sorry. I'm on my way now."

"*Violet.*" Lyn's tone cut through me. "It's okay."

"It's not." Fuck. I couldn't believe I was late for work.

"It really is. It's completely fine. It wasn't even…" Lyn sighed. "We aren't doing inventory. It was a surprise engagement party. Wedding party? It doesn't matter, because it's fine."

It did matter. Acid clawed its way up my throat. Had I known subconsciously, and blown it off? "I'm sorry."

"Stop," Lyn said harshly. "I get it. There's nothing to apologize for. You've been pushing yourself too hard. This isn't an offer anymore. I'm

running for it

giving you the next week off. If you come into work, I won't let you."

The time off sounded wonderful, but the circumstances filled me with a rancid mixture of anger and frustration. "But—"

"I'll talk to you in a week, Violet. Please, don't worry about it. I'm not mad. I'm just concerned. Get some rest."

I dropped my arm limply by my side. How did I let this happen?

"Violet." Hunter's concern penetrated the shell wrapping around me. "Hey." He placed a finger under my chin and lifted my head. "Owen told me what happened. Come on. We're going for lunch."

"I don't..." have time? I'd cleared my afternoon for work. That I'd forgotten.

Hunter tugged me toward his car. "Come on."

I sank into my seat and let him drive. He pulled into a drive through and ordered us sandwiches. Thankfully there was no greasy smell. I don't think I could have handled it. We headed toward his place, and then drove past his street.

"Where are we going?" I managed to ask.

"Just a little farther."

Not an answer. I sank lower in my seat, arms crossed.

A few minutes later, we reached a ridge that looked out over the valley. It was a turn-off tucked away from the rest of the world, where we could look down on them, but no one would see us.

Hunter put the car in park and turned to me. He forced my gaze to his. "You can't keep doing this."

"Doing what?" I didn't like the harsh tone.

Lines creased his forehead and he searched my face. "Your friends, all of us, need you. Don't doubt that for a second. But what you're doing, stretching yourself thin like this, it's not good for you."

"I don't have a choice. There are things that need to be done, and I promised to do them."

"I get that. And you don't have to do them alone. The people around you will help. I'll help."

But I'd promised to see them through. The idea of dropping anything, the way I had with this afternoon's promise to Lyn, made me sicker. "People are counting on me. You don't understand."

"I do understand." He traced gentle lines along my jaw as he held my chin. "I've been where you are."

I clenched my mouth shut, and braced myself for a story that proved he didn't get it at all.

"When I started college, I was working with my mom's organization—volunteering. And then Ramsey got into student government. It didn't matter that he was at a different school, I had so many ideas to help him. I was balancing all of that with being a freshman. With a course load I'd been told was too

running for it

much. I was running on less than four hours of sleep a night.”

I winced at a story that could have been mine, but kept my mouth shut.

“Things started to slip,” Hunter said. “Little things. I was late to an appointment here or there. I overbooked a few obligations. And then I let my mom down. And I missed getting some critical information to Ramsey. And it all came crashing down around me. I pushed so hard, I landed in the hospital for a few days.”

“Ouch.” I was sympathetic. Maybe he did get it. A little. “But that’s not me. I’m not that kind of physically ill. I’ve got this.”

Hunter’s frown deepened. “You do. Right now you’re keeping almost every ball in the air by yourself. How can I help?”

“I can’t ask you to do that. These are my obligations.”

“I’m not offering to do anything for you,” Hunter said. “You tell me what needs to be done, and I’ll do it.”

“I… I can’t.”

He gripped my chin harder, and stared me down with a fierceness that stole my breath. “This is destroying you. I won’t make a plan to ease up your workload, but you have to.”

"The plan is, I'll take the week Lyn gave me, make sure everything else is in order at the shelter, and then I won't miss any more appointments."

"That's not what I mean."

It didn't matter. It was the best I had.

Chapter Twenty-Two

When I woke up in the morning, I almost felt worse than after that last hangover. The one where my world fell apart. My clock said it after eight in the morning. I didn't remember the last time I'd slept so late.

Besides Vegas.

I peeled myself out of bed. Every inch of me was exhausted. Things were strained last night with Hunter. We'd brought the sandwiches home. I ate with him, to prove I was taking his advice and trying to relax, but I hadn't known what to say.

As I stumbled across the room, something caught my eye. A folder sitting near my closed bedroom door. There was a Post-it note on top, with Hunter's neat script handwriting

Sorry I missed you before work. We'll talk about this, I promise. I wanted you to know they exist.

I opened the folder. The top page was a court document with Hunter and my names at the top, and *PETITION FOR DIVORCE* underneath.

So, there was that. I guess it made sense. We didn't have to hide anything from his family.

I didn't want to follow any trains of thought about the paperwork, and I didn't know what to do with myself. I told Hunter I'd make a plan, but I was so tired. My bed called my name, and I hated myself as I climbed back under the covers, but I also needed to lie back down.

My phone ringing dragged me back go consciousness. Somehow it was almost two in the afternoon. I forced the sleep away as best I could, and answered. "Hello?"

"Hey, Taffy." Ramsey's greeting danced over me, drawing me awake better than any coffee.

I should ask him not to call me that, but I was too happy to hear his voice. "Hey."

"I don't like the way we left things the other night. The way we keep leaving them."

I didn't either. "But I hate the alternative, too. Not the being with you part. Everything else."

"I get it. And I didn't call to rehash. We each know where the other stands."

And yet, neither of us was budging. "What's up?" I couldn't handle any sort of emotional or business conversation right now.

"I called to talk."

When people said that, it was rarely a good thing. "About...?"

running for it

"I don't care. Wow." Ramsey chuckled. "That came out wrong. I should say *anything*. I get to see Hunter every day, but I miss you. I had you back for such a short amount of time, and now you're just out of reach. I called to hear your voice."

My heart cracked. So much for not getting emotional. "You're not going to ask what I'm wearing, then?" I tried to tease. It was enough to lift my mood a notch.

"Now that you mention it…" Ramsey's smooth tone buoyed me further.

"Nope. Missed your chance." My playfulness slipped out more easily than I expected.

"Hmm…" His low hum rolled over and through me. "I'll tell you what I'm wearing. Suit. Tie. Wingtips."

And I had no doubt he looked sexy as fuck. "You're begging for it in an outfit like that."

"I don't beg. You know me better than that." Something clanged with Ramsey's voice.

Was that… "Why do I hear slot machines?"

"I just finished lunch with Dottie."

"In Las Vegas? Don't we have a thing tonight?" I shouldn't have said anything. Now I was dreading another fundraiser.

"We do. And I'll be back before then."

The conversation had taken a suspicious turn. "What so important in Las Vegas that you have to do it in person?" Did I have a right to ask that? I didn't care. Curiosity won out.

"It's a surprise."

I grasped for a response.

"I know you hate surprises," Ramsey said quickly. "I'll tell you about this one as soon as I'm able, and I promise it's good."

"I hope so. I can't take any more bad ones."

"I promise." Ramsey repeated. "I'll see you tonight?'

He and Hunter would be the highlight of my evening. "Bright and smiling on my man's arm," I said.

"*My* man. I'd only share with you."

I smiled. "Don't I feel special."

"You should. You always should. And I'm serious."

I stumbled over his meaning. "You're giving me permission to fall in love with my husband? So generous." My teasing felt flat.

"No," Ramsey said. "Even I can't stop something like that. I'm giving you permission to fuck my boyfriend."

"Did I mention how generous you are?" Despite parrying the comments, my mind was racing along the potential. Clinging to a desire I'd barely dared skim the surface of, as images teased me of being wrapped up in Hunter. Of admitting there was more

running for it

of a connection to our sex. Of not having to assume he'd be gone in the morning.

Then the reality of last night brought the fantasy crashing down around me. "Pretty sure I've burned that bridge. He's asking for things from me I can't give."

"That doesn't sound familiar at all." Sarcasm laced Ramsey's reply. "You have your limits and he has his."

Was he really comparing my desire to not drop my obligations to his cavern of secrets? "But unlike me, his aren't reasonable."

"Hunter will do the impossible for someone he cares about," Ramsey said. "But he won't watch them destroy themselves. That's not unreasonable."

What happened to our angsty-light conversation? "I'm not—"

"Have this talk with him. But I know you'll work it out."

"How are you so certain?"

"Because I love you both, and I have excellent taste in people."

There were so many holes in that reply, I didn't know where to start picking it apart. I also didn't want to. "I don't have your confidence."

"So borrow some of mine." Ramsey's voice went muffled for a moment, as he talked to someone else, and then he was back. "I'm so sorry. I have to run. I miss you Taffy. Always when you're not around."

I shouldn't say it. The words would hurt. But holding them inside didn't make them any less painful. "I miss you too."

"We'll make this right, I promise."

I didn't know if we could, but as we disconnected I needed him to be right.

I sat on the bed for the longest time, staring at my phone. What was I supposed to do with my afternoon? If I checked in on the contractors at the shelter again, they'd probably bar me from the premises. I'd finished the month's paperwork.

Was it too early to get ready for the fundraiser tonight? It was a more casual event, so I didn't have to do the whole evening gown and heels thing.

Even though I was staying in the guest room, the bathroom was much larger than the one in my apartment. I'd been so busy, I hadn't had a chance to try out the large tub. It would be a shame to move out and not give it a whirl at least once.

Move out, the words soured in my gut, so I ignored them and ran a bath instead. The water was a half notch above comfortable when I dipped my hand in. *Perfect*. I stripped off my clothes and slipped into the water.

The heat wrapped around me, yanking me toward serenity. Was I really fighting relaxation?

running for it

Hunter's and Ramsey's words bounced in my head, demanding I give them attention.

Why couldn't I just chill for a few hours? A question that extended far beyond the walls of this room and this moment.

I let Lyn down yesterday. Sure, it was a party, but what if it had been work? Or Luna needing something? Or a crisis with one of the kids? Not a basement flooding crisis, but the kind of crisis my sister had gone through.

If I pushed myself to a crash, to hospitalization, I couldn't be there for them.

Or yourself, I swore that was Hunter's voice in my head.

I sank lower in the water, until my head from the nose up was the only thing not submerged. If I relaxed now, what would happen? Anything worse than if I didn't?

No. In fact, if something did come up, I could probably deal with it better.

Why did admitting that feel like surrender?

I struggled with logic versus instinct as I soaked. After the bath, I took my time stripping off the blue nail polish from two weeks ago and doing my hair. Hurrying through either meant waiting, and either could be dropped if someone called.

No one did.

Hunter got home a little after five, and I was sitting on the couch with the divorce papers on the coffee table.

He looked between them and me. "You want to do this now."

"Did you think I'd want to wait?"

He shook his head. "Tell me what you're thinking."

So. Many. Things. I doubted he wanted a dissertation. Then again, Hunter would probably listen to me spew out every single thought I'd had since I woke up. "You first."

"I already had a turn." He crossed the room and stopped a few feet away, keeping the table and the paperwork between us.

"I can't just turn off my obligations."

"You don't have to. I'd never ask that. I want you to take the first step toward making sure you're as taken care of as everyone you're looking out for."

It sounded so simple. More when he said it than when I'd made the argument with myself. "If I stop..." What? The world hadn't ended today. I felt better rested than in weeks.

"You're not stopping. You're doing a risk assessment and re-prioritizing." Of course he had to make sense about it all.

running for it

Was I ready for that? "I think we got off-track. This is about the—" divorce. I couldn't say it, so I gestured to the paperwork.

"Agreed. We can't have one conversation without the other. Unless you're ready to sign that paperwork." Hunter's confident tone wavered.

He was holding a marriage I hadn't wanted over my head to force me to change who I was. No. That was the wrong way to look at it, and he'd made sure to say so.

"All right, I'll go first." Hunter came around the table and took the spot next to me. He cupped my face between his palms. "I don't think I'm ready to sign the paperwork. I'm not saying I'd propose— yet—if we had a chance to do things differently, but we didn't. *What if* isn't part of the equation."

Each stroke of his thumb along my cheekbone sent a fissure of comfort through me. He searched my face. "I've always liked you," he said. "You make Ramsey smile, but that's not the only reason or even the main reason. You're smart. You're witty. You're fun as hell to hang with. You've always been a good friend, and even though it meant I got Ramsey, I didn't like when the two of you split because it meant you were gone. But you're not competition. These last few weeks have forced me to admit I love you, Violet."

The words sang to my heart, and pulled a similar declaration to the surface. I opened my mouth.

Hunter pressed a thumb to my lips. "But I also won't watch you destroy yourself, because you think it's helpful to others." He let me go.

Chapter Twenty-Three

Hunter loved me.

But he wanted to change me.

No. He wanted to help me. If I let myself trip over the last few weeks, which I had to do to process this, I could see how bad things were. That this wasn't the beginning of a downward slope, I'd been plummeting toward the bottom of a ravine of taking on way too much before the boiler failed at the shelter.

I also saw Hunter, a bright spot of sanity and warmth in the midst of it all. Ramsey was there too. Just out of reach. I wanted more of both when I looked back, and when I looked forward.

"I love you, too." It was so much easier to say that than I expected. My heart fluttered just as much speaking the words as it did hearing them. "And I'm scared of making this change you're talking about, but I'm terrified of staying on the path I'm on."

Hunter brushed his lips over mine. "I'm here for you. Everything I said stands."

"And Ramsey?" It was an unformed question. It could mean a million things to either of us. "Technically he and I are still broken up."

"He didn't tell me what he's doing in Vegas, but he promised it would fix things. I trust him. Can we go back to us?"

We could. Now that I knew I wasn't trading one guy for another. "Yes."

Hunter's kiss was so tender, it was heartbreaking. Or the opposite. Was *heartmending* a thing? I was making it thing, because the cracks in mine were sealing and vanishing.

His feathered kisses along my lips and face and neck stole my breath. I didn't know what to do besides grip his shirt in both fists and hold on tight.

Kisses blended into more. Tentative touches up my stomach, under my shirt. Groping through my bra and teasing my nipples as I stroked his erection through his slacks. It was a drawn out make-out session that put any I'd been a part of when I was younger to shame. This wasn't desperate pawing, it was a methodical build-up of pleasure.

Hunter pressed his lips to the hollow below my ear. "Do you remember what I said about fucking you?"

"That you like it?"

running for it

"Such an understatement. Memories of being buried inside you and wrapped around you haunt my dreams."

I flushed at the strength in his words. "You're so poetic," I said.

"You expected anything else? I'm torn between spending the night devouring you, and the fact that we have someplace to be. If I ask you to join me in the shower, will it ruin your hair?"

I gave him a look that I hoped conveyed *ask me instead if I care.* "I'd love to join you in the shower."

Hunter led me into the master suite bathroom, which made the one in my room look tiny. The large walk-in shower only took up a small corner of the room, and there was plenty of space for two behind the glass. He turned on the water, and we stripped off our clothes.

He tested the water a few times before finally tugging me under the stream with him, and sliding the door shut to close us off from the rest of the world. He pressed his chest to my back to kiss along my shoulders and neck while he glided his hands up my stomach to cup my breasts.

"You've raised the bar on foreplay." My teasing was breathy. Each new touch was fresh and tantalizing.

"You deserve that and more."

As the water sluiced over us, Hunter glided his hands along my every curve, teasing and caressing until I was slick from the build-up.

He slipped his fingers between my legs, teasing my pussy, then hooked his hand under my knee to plant my foot on the seat in the corner. Yeah, he had a built-in seat in his shower.

I leaned forward as he dragged the head of his cock along my ass cheek, and then my slit. He penetrated me with a long groan that sent a shiver of delight through me. He didn't move inside me, though.

The water stopped striking my skin, and a moment later, he was holding the shower head between my legs. "Tell me when I hit the right spot," he said.

I guided the pulsating water into place, and a shudder ran through me as the steady stream hit my clit.

"Hold this in place." Hunter handed me the shower nozzle. He gripped my hips, and then he was pounding inside me. Hard. Fast. Digging his fingers into my water-slicked skin.

The combination of sensations built fast, after the slow path we'd taken to get here, and my body tensed in anticipation. Every muscle coiled, waiting for release. Needing it.

running for it

And then orgasm crashed around me, from my core, from Hunter's frantic pace. From everywhere. I clenched around his cock, lost in the pleasure, and milking him.

"Fuck, Violet." He squeezed me harder. The pounding reached frenetic, even as I let the shower nozzle fall away. Hunter spilled inside me, his groan loud and intoxicating when he came.

As he slowed to a stop, neither of us moved for several moments. Water struck our shins. He pressed his lips into my shoulder and pulled me back into him.

"You're incredible in so many ways, Violet."

I leaned more weight against him. "I could say the same to you. Don't take this wrong, but you're officially my favorite mistake."

"I love it." He laughed.

We took our time soaping up and rinsing each other clean. It was hard to move quickly when every other touch was followed up with a kiss. We finally managed to step out of the shower, and get ready for the evening.

The drive there passed in a haze of me thinking about how amazing this was. I almost managed to ignore the nagging voice reminding me I needed this with Ramsey, too, to feel complete. Did that make me greedy? I didn't care. I wanted them both anyway.

Tonight's fundraiser was in another convention room, in another hotel. The only thing that distinguished most of these from each other was the color of the tablecloths. Pink this time—a perfect match to my flush every time I thought about Hunter.

I clung to him from the moment we arrived. We looked like the perfect, loving couple. It came naturally to have him whispering in my ear. To laugh at his comments. To exchange little kisses. Tonight it was because of this fresh commitment we had, but even before, it felt right to be close to him. To fall into this role.

It took more than an hour for both us and Ramsey to be free enough to approach each other. As the three of us headed toward a less crowded part of the room, Debbie joined Ramsey.

If she pulled him away for hours again, I'd be so furious. I didn't care whether or not I had the right to be.

It didn't look like she was saying anything to him, but his flat expression spoke volumes given he'd been smiling and laughing all night.

"I need to speak with the three of you," Debbie said as soon as Hunter and I were within hearing range. "It's not a request."

Bossy much?

Ramsey gave a terse nod. "All right."

running for it

Did he know what was going on? This wasn't his *surprise* was it? If so, it was off to a shitty start.

We followed Debbie down the hallway, to an empty conference room. She flipped on a switch, which illuminated just enough space to make things eerie, and closed the door behind us.

"What?" Ramsey asked sharply.

Debbie was focused on me, with a disgust in her gaze that made my skin crawl. "I can't believe you're a part of this," she said. "This marriage is a scam, and that's the least horrible thing about what's going on here. It's bad enough that Ramsey is hiding that he's fucking another man. But you? Absolutely disgusting that you'd demean yourself to hide their secret, given who you are. Do the kids at that shelter know?"

"Excuse me?" I could match disgust with anger, and then raise the ante to fury. "Did you—"

Ramsey settled a hand on my arm, and silenced me with a look.

"My personal life is none of your fucking business." His voice was hard.

"It is if you want to win this race, and the next one." Debbie stepped closer until she was in Ramsey's face. "This is the kind of bullshit behavior that makes losers, and I will *not* work for someone who's not interested in being the best."

Ramsey's expression went flat. "I see." His voice was stony. I'd rarely seen him like this—so furious he'd bottled the rage to use for later. "You're right, Debbie." There was no intonation in his voice. He was half a step from being a computerized voice. "I'll handle things tonight, and we'll talk in the morning."

Debbie blinked several times—was she surprised or something else? "Okay. I'll prepare a press re—"

"You won't do anything. We'll talk in the morning means we'll talk in the morning, and in the meantime, you'll keep all of your employment agreements in mind." Ramsey opened the door. "I assume you can find your own way back to the event."

"Yes. Thank you."

So that was what it took to shut up Debbie.

As she left, Hunter let out a long puff of air. "Wow."

Ramsey's chuckle was strained. "I'm done for the night. Think anyone would notice if we cut out early?"

"It's not your event," Hunter said. "No one will care."

"Are you sure she won't talk tonight?" How was I the only one worried about things falling apart if we walked away?

running for it

Ramsey nodded. "If she does, every Miller lawyer in the universe will be riding her ass. But worse, no one will let her work their campaign again. The *exposing us* threat is a bluff."

"How can you be so sure?"

"Because I've been watching this game play out far longer than I care for. Meet back at your place?" Ramsey looked between us.

Because it was our place. Hunter's and mine. The drive home would have been tense, if Hunter hadn't settled his hand on mine every chance he got.

Ramsey was already inside when we arrived. I wasn't surprised he had a key, but I did wonder how he got here so much sooner than we did. Hard to shave even a few minutes off a fifteen minute drive.

The instant Hunter closed the door, Ramsey crossed the room in a few long strides, grabbed a fistful of Hunter's shirt, and yanked him close, crushing their mouths together. They radiated desire and adoration.

I'd never watched anything hotter.

They broke apart with a duet of groans, but didn't move away from each other. Ramsey slid his hand to the back of Hunter's head, holding the two of them together. "I can't keep this up," Ramsey growled. "Two weeks is too long. There's no way I can stay away from you for nine months."

"Same." Hunter's reply was a bittersweet blend of need and sadness.

I should feel like an intruder right now. An interloper in an otherwise beautiful connection, but instead I was grateful to be a part of it. This didn't make me doubt what I had with either of them, and it reminded me they trusted me enough to let me be a part of it.

Still, it left my lips lonely and reminded me that Ramsey and I had a massive unresolved issue that kept us from having that.

Ramsey trailed his fingers forward to Hunter's jaw, brushing over his lips before finally dropping the touch and turning to me.

The intensity in Ramsey's gaze, the way he focused on only me, sparked through me. "I can't watch the two of you side-by-side and not be a part of it," Ramsey said. "You are so many amazing things, Taffy, but you're absolute shit at faking it."

"I'm not faking this." There it was. Telling Ramsey—confirming what he should already suspect—made my relationship with Hunter more real.

"Exactly." Ramsey flexed his fingers. He was so close, but didn't reach out.

I was both grateful and disappointed, because I wouldn't be able to tell him *no*. "So...?"

running for it

"You're right." The same thing he'd said to Debbie earlier, but in a vastly different tone. This was resignation and acceptance and hope. "I'm tired of this. Of missing Hunter. Of missing *you*. Of hiding who I love. Of trying to figure out what a future looks like if I have to tell more and more lies to keep our secrets. The public can accept who I am, or..."

"Or...? You'll move on? Just like that?" I needed to hear more. Right now, this was the chocolate brownie meant to sate a craving that was a day too old to be fresh.

Ramsey shook his head. "There's no *just* here. I'm resetting my priorities, and there are other places I can make a difference that won't require me to make this kind of compromise." He reached back to pull Hunter closer. "This decision isn't mine alone, though. I'm done asking the two of you to stay married, but I do need your permission to talk about us publicly. Otherwise, I'll leave your names out of it as much as I can."

"You'd better fucking not." Hunter's voice was hard. "You are *never* leaving my name out of your life again."

The two of them were *so* good together.

And I still hadn't been kissed. "What are you going to do? Tell the world *hey, I'm in an consensual relationship with a woman and another man. Accept it or suck it.*"

Ramsey laughed. A genuine, throaty sound. "Tempting, but I was thinking only if someone asked. I was leaning more toward telling the world I'm not straight, and that any other information about my personal life is that—personal."

"And if they push for details?" The way I was. This was too good to be true, but I really needed his commitment to the truth to be real. "If Hunter's name comes up? If mine does? If they want to know about our marriage?"

"Then I'll answer their questions. I won't lie. I need you back, Taffy." Ramsey traced a thumb over my bottom lip, drawing a soft gasp.

"I need that too." *Goddess* it felt incredible to say that.

Ramsey claimed my mouth hungrily, in an all-consuming kiss. He bit my bottom lip. Teased my tongue with his. Nibbled along my skin until my lips were swollen and tender and eager for more.

Chapter Twenty-Four

"What was in Vegas today?" I asked Ramsey between hungry kisses.

He sank his teeth into my shoulder. "A new future."

"No." I groaned into the delicious sting. "No more riddles or surprises. How does it help us?"

He pulled away to look at me. "Tomorrow morning, Hunter is going to fire Debbie. He's going to do this as I'm holding a press conference to withdraw from the senate race."

"Oh." Not what I expected, but maybe I should have. Ramsey coming out was unlikely to end his career, but everything else about our relationship may not go over so well, and it wouldn't stay hidden if we weren't actively hiding it. "But… What about making a difference? Being made for this?" Every other reason he'd given me over the years for why he had to behave.

"I've been thinking about what you said. All of it, but specifically what you said about the pop-up event we did with Dottie. I talked to her today, to her lawyer, and financial adviser, about starting a charitable foundation to help shelters like yours. To bolster them. To build more of them. I'm going to head the entire thing, work my connections to grow it, and I'm hoping to God that Hunter will help me with the administrative details." Ramsey finished with a satisfied grin.

"Well, apparently my boss is quitting his job tomorrow," Hunter said. "So I do have an opening in my schedule."

Ramsey turned his head long enough to give Hunter a quick kiss. "You're hired." Ramsey turned back to me. "That's the surprise. That's how I fix things. I'd do it anyway. You were right, it's how I can make a difference. But I'm hoping you'll stick around to see things in action. With me."

"I will." I couldn't fight my smile.

Ramsey gripped the back of my neck with a strength and possession that lit my soul on fire. "I love you, Violet. Every day you're not here, every day for the past few years, I've missed you." He drew his tongue up the side of my neck, to nip my earlobe. "I'm not letting you go again. Either of you."

"Is this a good or a bad time to tell you we decided not to go through with the divorce?" I didn't want to ruin the moment, but since we were implying long-term here, and I wanted exactly that, someone should bring it up.

running for it

Ramsey kissed along the shell of my ear. "I told you," somehow he made a whisper sound like a command, "I'll only share with you. With him. But you're both mine."

As he said *mine* he bit my neck. I'd be covered in marks soon, and the idea made desire throb between my thighs. "I love you too. Intensely. Completely. From now until forever."

"I want something from you," Ramsey growled against my skin.

"Anything."

"I want you on the couch, naked, fingering your pussy while I suck my boyfriend's cock."

I smiled through my flush. "You're such a charmer."

He tangled his fingers in my hair and tugged. "Damn right I am." He crushed his mouth to mine, stealing my breath. Pouring intensity and desire into the connection that flowed between us. "Naked and playing with yourself. *Now.*"

Ramsey let me go and I stepped away. I felt a bit silly taking off my clothes like this. Was I supposed to do something sensual? Dance? Just tearing them off all random-like didn't feel right.

I was deliberate about stripping my sweater over my head. When the knit material cleared my eyes, and I saw two gazes focused on me, confidence surged inside. I shimmied out of my slacks. Made a little show of taking off my bra and pushing my panties to the ground, and settled on the couch.

Hunter and Ramsey were still staring at me.

"Well?" I asked.

Ramsey shrugged. "Well?"

"You're supposed to be the show," I said.

He grinned. "Fair point." He turned back to Hunter and crushed their mouths together in a drawn-out, groan-inducing kiss.

I felt the ghost of fingers and lips gliding over me each time they moved against each other, and it clenched around me with desire.

Ramsey unbuckled Hunter's belt with a practiced flick of the wrist, and whipped it free from its loops with a sharp *crack* that sent shivers through me. Then they were kissing again. Bodies molded to each other. Mouths hungrily devouring each other's grunts. Ramsey gripping Hunter's erection through his pants.

The heat and intensity that flowed between them sparked over me. I was a part of that connection, and that was as enticing as every grope and touch.

I glided my hands over my torso, touching lightly enough to tantalize over my breast, my stomach, and my inner thighs. I wanted that feeling

running for it

of skin on skin, but I wanted to draw out this moment of voyeurism.

Ramsey undid Hunter's trousers and lowered himself to his knees as he freed Hunter.

Hunter's groan, when Ramsey took him in his mouth, drew a similar sound from me.

Why did I have to get naked to watch the show? Did I care? Not really, given how incredible the watching was. Hunter half-closed his eyes and leaned his head back as Ramsey bobbed his head. Sucking. Licking. Stroking Hunter's balls.

I spread my legs and slipped my fingers to tease my opening and draw out the slickness. I spread my juices up and down, gliding along my pussy as Hunter's groans grew more stuttered. Less controlled.

I dipped my fingers inside me, and reached for my clit with my other hand. I pumped and stroked faster in time with the bob of Ramsey's head. I saw the tension coiling through Hunter. He was close, and I wanted to see his pleasure when he came.

Hunter's face screwed up, and his grunts were stuttered. He was fucking Ramsey's face harder and harder, until he paused. Shuddered. Sagged.

I let myself come, with Hunter's pleased posture burned in my mind. I closed my eyes and my head fell back as pleasure and climax wrapped around me. My orgasm tapered off, and I struggled to find my breath.

Hunter's mouth closed over mine, startling me. He was still panting too, teasing my lips as we gave each other life.

He broke away, and as Ramsey grabbed my wrist, I let my eyelids flicker open. Ramsey held my gaze as he sucked my fingers clean, each lick sending a shudder of delight through me.

When Ramsey finished, he moved my hand to his waist. "Take out my cock and stroke it."

His command and confidence stoked my need. I scooted to the edge of the cushion and did as ordered, freeing him. Wrapping my hand around his shaft. Holding his gaze as I stroked lightly. I teased my thumb over the head and smeared a drop of precum, and he shuddered.

Ramsey pulled my hand away and tugged me to my feet. "Do you remember the night we met?"

"Vividly."

"The one thing I desperately wanted that night was to pull you into my lap and fuck you." Ramsey sat on the couch, turned my back to him, and guided me toward his lap. As I lowered myself, he slid inside me. He wrapped his arms around me and pulled me into his chest, burying himself to the hilt and stretching me out in the best way possible.

running for it

He kissed along the back of my neck as he rocked inside me.

Hunter knelt in front of me and my anticipation spiked. He pressed his face between my legs licking me and Ramsey at the same time. Hunter teased my clit with his tongue and devoured my pussy while Ramsey built to slow, steady pace.

They both worked me, the pressure and pleasure building inside me, growing, blooming, driving my senses wild, until I came hard. I rode the wave of orgasm, enjoying every fresh sensation.

Ramsey pounded harder. Hunter pulled away and joined us on the couch, to press his lips to mine, sharing my taste with me. To kiss Ramsey. To tease my nipples.

Ramsey's thrusting grew to a frantic pace, pounding against me. His grunts and grip were familiar and right. He spilled inside me with a drawn-out groan.

As we all came to a stop, the world seemed to pause with us. No one spoke as we leaned into each other. I was happy to be still and enjoy the closeness of the men I loved.

We moved to the bedroom, to collapse in an exhausted but pleased pile on Hunter's bed. He and I each rested our heads on Ramsey's chest.

"So, the two of you…" Ramsey's voice rumbled through me. "Should I be jealous?" His tone was light.

"Mister I Don't Share Well?" Hunter scoffed. "Can you be anything but?"

I laughed. "This coming from the guy who said he wouldn't share his man."

"Ah." Hunter's bravado faded. "You remember that."

My smile wouldn't leave as I snuggled closer to Ramsey. "Yes. The two of us. The three of us, technically."

"I couldn't have planned it better," Ramsey said.

"Which is why you have me." Hunter propped himself up on one elbow.

I shifted my position enough so I could see him without straining. "While I see your point, you couldn't have planned it any better, either."

Hunter raised an eyebrow. "Oh?"

"Nope. Because it doesn't get better." I sighed.

Ramsey tilted his head up to kiss the tip of my nose. "You're a sap sometimes. I love it. Especially when it means you admitting I was right."

I snorted with laughter. "You were *so* not right. But things worked out in spite of that."

"Do I get to wear the ring?" Hunter's change of subject was blatant.

running for it

"Ravyn gets to wear the ring. I gave it to her yesterday, with Dottie's blessing. This way it stays in the family, and she can wear it no matter who she ends up with," Ramsey said.

"CoughBenCough." Hunter's words ran together. Ben and Ravyn were BFF's forever, the same way Ramsey and Hunter had been, and both of their families expected they'd end up together.

Ramsey clucked. "Don't let her hear you say that."

"You still weren't right." I'd let the subject drop now. I just had to get in one last word.

Ramsey shifted quickly, displacing me, and I squealed in surprise. He rolled enough to pin me to the mattress, his chest pressing into mine. "Take it back."

I stared back stubbornly. "Make me."

"Nope. Never." He tilted his head and brushed his lips over mine. "We're all here because this is where we want to be."

I wouldn't—couldn't—argue that. This really was better than I could have imagined, being back with Ramsey. Realizing how much Hunter meant to me. Life was incredible.

Epilogue

Six Months Later
Hunter

There were a lot of things I loved about Violet. One of the simpler ones was the fantastic company she provided when Ramsey was on stage. This afternoon he was cutting the ribbon on the first of many new shelters his foundation brought to life.

Violet's hand was nestled in mine and her head rested against my shoulder, as we stood at the back of the crowed, watching Ramsey on a temporary platform in front of a motel that had been converted. For the last several months, I'd pushed around all the figures and paperwork and kept all the cogs moving to make it happen.

The house Violet managed was fantastic—small, structured and friendly—but it only held so many people. This place would give a similar experience to dozens more homeless youth who needed stability, shelter, and a home.

Ramsey was telling the audience something similar, minus the Violet bits, but in snappier words

running for it

that would make good sound bites and be highly quotable.

The faint smile on Violet's face was there more often than not these days. While Ramsey would insist in jest, probably, that it was because she was getting some incredible dick on a regular basis, I knew it was because she was getting better at how she took things on.

It didn't hurt either that my both of my parents had welcomed her and Ramsey into the family with open arms. When we finally had dinner with Mom, and didn't have to lie about the marriage being real, she and Violet got along splendidly. And Dad was still hanging on. Tough old bastard.

As Ramsey finished his speech and cut the ribbon, I tugged Violet away from the gathering and into an empty part of the shelter. It would be open for business next week, but for now, only certain parts of the building were available for photo ops. That was where Ramsey would be.

I'd rather steer clear of the cameras. I led her to the main administrator's office.

"You show me the sexiest things," she teased as we stepped into the room.

"Later, if you're good, I'll let you watch me create Excel formulas."

Violet laughed and pretended to swoon. "I'm not sure I could handle the heat."

I settled into the chair behind the desk and pulled her into my lap. She rested her head on my shoulder, palm resting on my heart. The only thing that would make this moment more perfect would be if Ramsey were here with us.

When Violet and Ramsey broke up a few years ago, when I finally let myself admit how I felt about him, I'd assumed we'd live a life that swung wildly between public and private. I didn't like the idea, but he was worth it.

This was so much better, though. So much more than I'd ever dared imagine. Married to an amazing woman. Committed to an incredible man. Giving others a chance at the same. If I'd wished on a magic lamp, I couldn't have come up with a more perfect scenario.

Ramsey

I took the press on a brief tour of the new shelter. Mostly the common areas. This was our experiment with this kind of project, and it went well. Starting tomorrow, we were spinning up several more projects like this, in larger cities around the country that didn't have many options for LGBTQ+ youth.

For the next forty five minutes or so, we took photos, I answered more questions, and the mood

running for it

was light and cheery. My new press manager—Jake was as good as Debbie had been at getting the word out, and far less abrasive in the process—shooed everyone away.

I sent him home and went in search of Hunter and Violet. They hadn't told me where they'd be, besides *waiting*, but I could guess.

When I drew close to the main administrative office, I heard soft, familiar voices coming from inside. I summoned far more flair than I needed, and pushed the door open. "My best friend and my girlfriend. Wha—" My melodramatic exclamation trailed off. "You're cuddling."

Hunter looked up from Violet, who was sitting his lap. "You expected something else?" he asked.

"I expected you to christen the place. Fuck on the desk. Something."

Violet feigned shock. "But it's not our desk."

Hunter nodded, expression serious. "She's right. Isn't that kind of a creepy vibe?"

They were yanking my chain. They had to be. "Hotel sex is some of the best sex."

"This isn't a hotel anymore." Violet sounded serious, but her smirk was peeking through.

They were as much serious as they were joking. I loved it. "Right now it's mostly an empty building. The back of the Cayenne in the fast-food parking lot was more taboo than this place." That was a good fucking memory—a good memory of fucking? I'd watched Violet suck Hunter's cock. Fucked him while Hunter tasted himself on her lips. Watched her watching us as she pushed her new little black dress past her hips and fingered her pussy.

"It was after midnight, and the SUV windows are tinted." Apparently Hunter wasn't ready to let the joke drop.

I'd play along for about ten more seconds. "There are no windows in here and the door locks."

"But the door wasn't locked. Anyone could have walked in on us." Violet gave me a pointed glare, as if I were the case study for her point.

I was. "Which I think you wanted, since you didn't lock the door."

"Hang on, back up," Hunter said. "Are you arguing about the fact that we weren't having sex?"

"It's not an argument, it's an assessment."

Violet raised her eyebrows. "Of…?"

"Of which one of you I bend over that desk." I reached behind me and locked the door.

About Allyson Lindt

USA Today Bestselling Author Allyson Lindt is a full-time geek and a fuller-time author. She's found her own happily ever after, where she and her spouse call their furbabies their children. Coffee is her task-master and random tangents are her muse. When she's not writing, she's fangirling over the latest superhero movies. She likes her stories with sweet geekiness and heavy spice, and loves a sexy happily-ever-after. Because cubicle dwellers need love too. Learn more about Allyson's books, including signing up for her newsletter, by visiting http://www.allysonlindt.com.